FREE DOWNLOAD!

Check out
Amber Road's hit song

"beautiful girl"

You can
download the song for free
and learn more about the band at:

www.myspace.com/amberroad
www.dlgarfinkle.com

the **Band**

trading guys

DEBRA GARFINKLE

BERKLEY JAM, NEW YORK

A Parachute Press Book

THE BERKLEY PUBLISHING GROUP
Published by the Penguin Group
Penguin Group (USA) Inc.
375 Hudson Street, New York, New York 10014, USA
Penguin Group (Canada), 90 Eglinton Avenue East, Suite 700, Toronto, Ontario M4P 2Y3, Canada
(a division of Pearson Penguin Canada Inc.)
Penguin Books Ltd., 80 Strand, London WC2R 0RL, England
Penguin Group Ireland, 25 St. Stephen's Green, Dublin 2, Ireland (a division of Penguin Books Ltd.)
Penguin Group (Australia), 250 Camberwell Road, Camberwell, Victoria 3124, Australia
(a division of Pearson Australia Group Pty. Ltd.)
Penguin Books India Pvt. Ltd., 11 Community Centre, Panchsheel Park, New Delhi—110 017, India
Penguin Group (NZ), 67 Apollo Drive, Rosedale, North Shore 0745, Auckland, New Zealand
(a division of Pearson New Zealand Ltd.)
Penguin Books (South Africa) (Pty.) Ltd., 24 Sturdee Avenue, Rosebank, Johannesburg 2196,
South Africa

Penguin Books Ltd., Registered Offices: 80 Strand, London WC2R 0RL, England

This book is an original publication of The Berkley Publishing Group.

PRINTING HISTORY
Berkley JAM trade paperback edition / May 2007

Library of Congress Cataloging-in-Publication Data

Garfinkle, D. L. (Debra L.)
    The band : trading guys / Debra Garfinkle.—Berkley Jam trade paperback ed.
        p. cm.
    "A Parachute Press book."
    Summary: The friends in the band Amber Road always back each other up, onstage and off, but
just as they have a chance to be noticed as professional musicians, an impulsive game threatens to
tear them apart.
    ISBN 978-0-425-21513-5
    [1. Bands (Music)—Fiction.   2. Dating (Social customs)—Fiction.   3. Friendship—
Fiction.   4. Alcohol—Fiction.   5. California—Fiction.]   I. Title.

PZ7.G17975Ban 2007
[Fic]—dc22   2007000317

PRINTED IN THE UNITED STATES OF AMERICA

10 9 8 7 6 5 4 3 2 1

acknowledgments

Thank you to my husband, Jeff Garfinkle, who thought I was nuts for writing this novel but didn't complain. I also appreciate the real Mark and Aaron for letting me use their names. Mark is as kind as his namesake. Aaron is nothing like his, thank God. And Sarah, thank you for being you.

Thank you to the editors who took a chance on me and gave me valuable guidance: Dena Neusner, Susan Lurie, and Kate Seaver.

For their generous help in researching this novel, I thank April, Denny, Jessie, Becca, and Emily Holland, as well as Brandon Merchant, and especially Steve Guida, who is a much better person than the fictional Steve Guyda. You guys rock!

I don't want to be the most beautiful girl
I just want to be the most beautiful girl for you
I don't want to be the only one in the world
I just want to be the only one for you

one

Tracie Grant twirled her hair as she sat with her band-mates at Waves. She'd been to the club before at nighttime, sipping sodas, listening to other bands, dancing with her boyfriend, Carter, and her friends. But today would be a completely different experience. She and her bandmates would be auditioning to perform at Waves.

It was late afternoon and the nightclub wouldn't officially open for hours. Amber Road was among five bands trying out for the last slot in Thursday night's lineup. Getting the slot at Waves would elevate Tracie and her friends from an amateur garage band to professionals. They'd been rehearsing like crazy the last few weeks. They just *had* to score this gig.

Tracie gazed at the stage. The group auditioning now wore surly expressions and moved with clenched muscles as if they were mad at the world. Tracie couldn't imagine looking like that while playing her guitar. Her music brought her joy, not anger.

But right now she just felt fear. So much was riding on this audition, especially for her friend Mark, who had started the band and seemed to value it more than anything in his life. She couldn't let him down. She didn't want to let anyone down. But the way she felt now, she didn't know whether she could even climb up the stage steps without throwing up.

Next to her, her best friend, Sienna, touched her shoulder. "You seem really nervous, girl. Usually your pale complexion is so pretty, but today it almost looks ghostly."

"Thanks a lot," Tracie said. That was the problem with being so fair. Aside from her light skin, she had platinum blond hair with wispy bangs, and glassy blue eyes. "So I look all washed out?" she asked.

"No. Just worried," Sienna said.

"Listen to those guys from Crash." The band onstage was blasting hard rock songs in an eighties hair-band style. "They're good. I should be worried. You too, Sienna."

"I think we're better than they are," Sienna said. "Is Carter coming? I bet he'd calm you down."

"He has debate practice every Friday after school." Tracie held back a sigh. "He's going to the county championships on Sunday, so he's probably as nervous about the debate as I am about our audition today." On second thought, she doubted anyone could feel as nervous as she did right now.

"Knowing Carter, he'll win the debate title by a landslide. He's, like, Mr. Successful. And you're Mrs. Successful."

"If you say so."

"You're wearing that little smile on your face you always

get when we talk about Carter," Sienna said. "So I guess even if he's not here, he can comfort you in spirit."

Thinking about Carter did make her feel better. He was a good boyfriend, sweet, smart, steadfast, a terrific influence on her. They'd both already been accepted to Yale, early decision. She didn't think she would have studied so hard or done so many extracurricular activities if Carter hadn't encouraged her all these years. Plus, he was handsome too.

"Now you're positively beaming," Sienna said. "You and Carter are so perfect together."

They were, at least on paper. They studied together, volunteered together, filled out college applications together, did everything together except have sex. *That*, they had decided, should wait. Of course, they also made out together.

"Carter's a great guy. But it is nice to have a boyfriend who can come to all the band stuff," Sienna said. "Ah, the advantages of going out with a member of Amber Road. Right, Mark?"

"Right." Mark, sitting on the other side of Sienna, took her hand.

Tracie pointed at them. "Speaking of perfect couples." Sienna seemed totally content with Mark. She had liked him as soon as he walked into their AP English class for the first time last January, looking like a prepster in a long-sleeved polo shirt, khakis, and loafers, but with a Black Eyed Peas concert sweatshirt wrapped around his waist. A few weeks later, when he gave his oral poetry report on Bob Dylan, Sienna was practically swooning. She had asked him to the spring dance about a year ago, and they'd been together ever since.

They were a great couple. They both had dark good looks. Sienna was African-American, one of the few at their private school, and carried herself with pride. She had warm brown eyes and full lips and a voluptuous figure. Mark was Italian-American, with olive skin, large eyes that were almost black, and dark hair that Sienna always seemed to be running her fingers through. They both dressed conservatively. Sienna liked to joke that she was San Diego's only black preppie. And they were both very passionate about Amber Road. Tracie was happy her best friend had a boyfriend who seemed so ideal for her.

Crash finished its set and Tracie and her friends clapped politely.

Harry Darby, the club manager, stood up in the front row. The man looked silly. He was built like a sumo wrestler and compensated for the little hair on the top of his head with a long, thin brown beard hanging an inch off his chin. He wore an open shirt and gold chains, which might have been fashionable twenty-five years ago but *not* today.

Regardless of his looks, Tracie knew he was well respected in the San Diego music community. Mark had told everyone in Amber Road about Darby. Apparently, the guy had been running Waves for decades, and several famous bands had gotten their big breaks after Darby booked them. Waves was the only club in San Diego that held special auditions for new bands, reportedly because Darby was very dedicated to finding fresh talent. And the manager's decisions about when and how often the bands would perform could make a rising band sputter out or give a new band just the help it needed.

Everyone, the members of the five bands and friends in the audience, fell silent in deference to Darby. He pointed to a group of tattooed twentysomethings in the second row. "Thunder, you can perform next. Then you, over here." He pointed to Femme Fatale, an all-girl group Tracie had heard at a dance at the neighboring high school. She thought their looks far surpasses their musical ability. Darby pointed to Amber Road. "And then you'll go on after them."

Tracie bit her lip. She didn't know if she had the nerve to walk onstage, let alone jam on the guitar.

"Finally, Sandy Eggo." Darby pointed to the band behind them, hippie types with beards and tie-dyed shirts. "I'll make my decision today if you want to stick around a few minutes afterward," he said.

Once Darby sat down, Mark said, "Where in the world is Lily? We'll be on in minutes. Doesn't she know my heart is beating faster than George beats the drums?"

George Yee, seated in front of them, whipped his head around. "Hey, dude, I heard that. I'll challenge that little miserly heart of yours to a speed race anytime."

Good old George. He wasn't particularly smart or cute like Carter, but he was so goofy he always made Tracie smile too.

"No, thanks. You're killer on drums," Mark told him. "Hey, I hope you're all right playing the drum set onstage. I know you're used to your own equipment."

"Dude, I'm cool with any kind of stick I can bang on something to make a noise. Chill already."

Tracie wondered who was more anxious, she or Mark. Her stomach felt like it was caught in the middle of ten-foot surf.

"All right, I'll try to chill," Mark said. "But I sure would feel better if Lily were here."

"She'll be here," Sienna said. "She's always late. Knowing Lily, she'll stroll in, shaking her hips around, about a minute before we have to go on. So don't worry. Freaking out about scoring this gig won't get us anywhere."

Tracie clutched her churning stomach. She knew Sienna was right, but she still couldn't help being anxious bordering on petrified.

"I'm a little on edge, okay?" Mark said. "When was the last time we were waiting to audition at a cool club like Waves? Or at any club, anywhere, except for high school dances? Never."

"Even if Lily doesn't show, I know the songs." Sienna leaned close to Mark. "I *was* lead singer up until you gave her the job a few weeks ago."

It seemed like Sienna almost didn't want Lily to come.

Then Lily finally arrived. Even if Tracie and her bandmates hadn't been glancing at the entrance to Waves every few seconds, Lily would have been difficult to miss. She wore her bright red hair very long and her skimpy clothes without a bra.

Behind Lily was her twin brother, Aaron. Tracie's stomach started doing somersaults. She'd been jittery enough without having Aaron here too. How could she act cool when he was so hot? She could barely breathe when he was around.

"You're late," Sienna told Lily.

"Fashionably. You guys haven't been called onstage yet, have you?" Lily asked.

"That's not the point," Mark told her. "We were all supposed to be here a half hour ago."

"She's here, and you're just sitting around, so what's your point?" Aaron asked.

Tracie liked that he defended his sister. She also liked looking at him. Aaron Bouchet had a movie star's face and a gym rat's body. *You have a boyfriend,* she scolded herself. But looking at a cute guy wasn't the same as dating or fooling around with him, and what girl wouldn't like looking at Aaron? He was tall, at least six-two, and had muscles to match his height. He didn't so much walk as strut, as if he were the most important person in any room he entered. And there was his thick hair, a dark brown faintly streaked with gold, and his amazing eyes the color of espresso and the intensity of it too, that seemed to burn into her, stripping her bare.

She wondered if he looked at all girls that way. She hoped he didn't. Embarrassed by her thoughts, she made herself drop her gaze from Aaron's handsome face.

Wow. He was lifting up his strong arms and pulling his sweatshirt over his head. His T-shirt underneath was coming off too, and Tracie couldn't take her gaze from his lean stomach and six-pack and smooth, hairless torso.

"Whoops." He laughed. "Didn't want to take both shirts off." He pushed the bottom of his T-shirt down before lifting the sweatshirt over his head. He shook his hips while humming a stripper song.

Lily and Mark and George laughed.

"Tracie," Sienna whispered next to her. "Close your mouth."

She snapped it shut. How embarrassing. She'd been ogling Aaron as if he really were a stripper. Very tacky, made tackier by the fact that she had a boyfriend. *A great boyfriend*, she reminded herself. She stopped staring at Aaron's body, but couldn't help glancing at his face.

Aaron winked at her. At least Tracie thought that might be a wink.

Was it? Was he mocking her? Flirting with her? She turned her head away.

He sat down next to her. "Tracie, I can't wait to hear you get wild on your guitar."

Oh, God, he was definitely flirting with her.

"Her *boyfriend* is wild about her," Sienna said, practically shouting the word *boyfriend*.

"Where is he? He must be here somewhere," Aaron said.

Tracie turned toward him. She bet she was blushing. Another drawback of pale skin was that when she blushed, everyone knew it.

"Who wouldn't want to watch you perform onstage?" Aaron said.

She felt she had to defend Carter. "My boyfriend's at debate practice. He's got an important competition on Sunday."

"Nothing's more important than being there for your girl, especially when she's at one of the coolest clubs in San Diego," Aaron said. "If you were my girlfriend, I would never leave you alone."

"But I'm not. I'm Carter Branham's girlfriend," Tracie answered. "So I have to leave you alone."

As soon as she said it, she clapped her hand over her mouth. "I didn't mean it that way. I mean, I have to leave you. I mean, you have to leave me alone." Oh, God, she was just making things worse. In front of everyone too. She moved her hand up to cover her face. She couldn't even look at anyone.

"Tracie," Aaron said. "Do I make you uncomfortable? A little squirmy?"

"No!" It came out louder than she thought it would. *Thou doth protest too much,* she said to herself. *I've been reading too many Shakespeare romances, that's all. If Carter were here, I'd barely glance Aaron's way.* That's what she told herself, anyway.

The band onstage finished its set and Tracie clapped again, thankful for the diversion.

"We go on after the next band." Mark stood up. "Let's huddle. Everyone join me for a minute."

Lily, Tracie, and George came over, and the band members stood together in a circle. "Okay, captain, who do you want to hike the ball?" George joked. "Pass or run on this play?"

"Let's get serious," Mark said. "This is our biggest opportunity since we formed the band. Considering we've never performed in a club before, playing at Waves would be huge for us. This could lead to a steady gig here, or to bigger clubs, maybe even notice from big managers and record producers. We need to blow Harry Darby away today."

Mark's pep talk made Tracie feel even *more* nervous. This was such a big deal, and it meant so much to the rest of the band too.

"No problem," Lily said.

She didn't seem to be taking this seriously. Since when did she take anything seriously though?

"I don't think we have anything to worry about," Lily continued. "My music teacher took me aside yesterday and told me I have, like, one of the best natural voices she's ever heard. The manager will have to pick me."

"Pick *you*?" Sienna said. "Lily, this is a group audition. Everyone in Amber Road is auditioning, not just you."

Sienna's rebuke of Lily made Tracie feel even more anxious now. She knew that her friend's indignation wasn't just based on loyalty to Amber Road. Sienna was hurt that Mark, her boyfriend, had replaced her with Lily as lead singer a few weeks ago. The truth was that Lily had more talent. But truth could be painful, and how well a band got along could be just as important to its success as its members' individual talents. If a group didn't like each other offstage, the animosity would show in a disharmonious performance.

"Come on, girls." Mark looked worried. He put his arm around Sienna. "We're supposed to be supporting each other, not arguing with each other."

"Things are so different in Europe. Not so tense," Lily said. "Everyone just, like, lets other people be."

There went Lily, talking about Europe again. Sienna whispered to Tracie, "If Lily loves Europe so much, why doesn't she just move back there already?"

The band onstage finished their set. After the applause died down, Mark said, "Okay, Amber Road, we're up. Let's put any hard feelings aside and rock our hearts out."

"I don't have hard feelings," Tracie said. "Just feelings of total panic."

"You'll do great." Mark took her hand and led her onstage. The other members of Amber Road stormed past her. Why did everyone always seem more self-assured than Tracie?

"Let's knock 'em dead," Mark said as the sound guy finished checking their instruments and the mikes.

Mark poised his hands over his keyboard, called out, "Three, two, one, rock," and they began. As soon as Tracie played the first chord on her guitar, she got caught up in the sound and feel of the song rather than the stress of the audition. It always amazed her that with her fingers and a piece of wood and some metal strings, she could create fantastic art—rhythms and tones and moods. The vibe of the music totally vanquished her stage fright.

Their first song was from Shakira's latest CD. The vocal

was challenging, but Lily could sing practically anything. Tracie wished Lily would put a little more feeling into the song. It seemed more by-the-book than passionate. But her pitch was flawless and she showed off her amazing range.

It wasn't just Lily who was amazing. The other members of Amber Road totally had their game on. They didn't miss a note or play a bad key. And they all seemed as enthralled as Tracie was with being onstage and part of a group making great music.

She dared to peer at the audience. Even though it was made up of people from other bands and their friends, a lot of them were cheering for Amber Road. Yes!

Her gaze fell on Aaron. He was staring at her intently. Not at his sister Lily or at anyone else. His eyes were locked on Tracie.

She smiled at him. The thought of Carter might induce a little unconscious smile, but the sight of Aaron, with his dark eyes and sexy smile, brought on a big, excited grin.

And he smiled right back at her.

Stop flirting, Tracie told herself. *Put your energy into the performance.* She decided to go for it, to show Aaron she was worth staring at, that she was more than just the sweet, timid honor student she often felt like. For the first time ever, she moved onstage with total abandon. She strutted all around the wooden platform with her guitar, stomping her feet and shaking her hips, wailing on her guitar solo, giving it her all and giving Aaron a show that she had performed before only in front of her bedroom mirror.

At the end of the song, Sienna and Tracie high-fived each other. Obviously, Sienna thought they had nailed it too. They had. Sienna's strong rhythms on bass guitar had accompanied Tracie's lead guitar perfectly. Everyone in Amber Road had been awesome. The band whooped and jumped and bowed. Aaron put his hand over his heart and mouthed *Wow*, and Tracie's grin filled her face.

two

The second and last song was "Rock It Like a Rocket," which Mark had written a few months ago. To Mark, there was nothing better than hearing something he'd created come alive onstage. And Amber Road performed the song wonderfully today. Lily, Sienna, and Mark sang with vitality and perfect harmony from the very first line, a great relief after Lily and Sienna's squabble a few minutes ago. George went wild on the drums, the fast beat making everyone even more pumped up.

Lily's vocals soared above the others', and her appearance was almost as remarkable as her singing ability. Her wavy red hair cascaded down her back like an ocean on fire, her bright blue eyes sparkled as if she were imagining something fantastic, her breasts were only partly covered by a tight tank top and no bra, her legs seemed to go on forever, and her long thin arms were lined with metallic bracelets. She looked totally exotic.

Even the way Lily moved her body was exotic. It was in rhythm to the music, but also wild and sensual, as if she were trying to seduce every male in the audience. And Mark imagined that most of the guys watching her were seduced. If he weren't with Sienna—*happily with her,* he reminded himself—he too might be crazy for Lily.

She was a great addition to the band. Just being onstage with Lily and her brazen spirit made Mark play with more passion. The entire band was bursting with energy. Amber Road had never performed better. Once the set came to a close, the group left the stage sweaty and tired, but also grinning and pumping their fists.

Mark was so proud of them, Lily especially. Everyone in Amber Road was good, but Lily's voice was dazzling—strong and sultry. Sometimes Mark wished Lily would sing with more passion, but otherwise, her vocals were fantastic. He knew he'd made the right decision to substitute Lily as lead singer in Sienna's place. But even with Amber Road in top form today, Mark wasn't sure if they'd be chosen as the very best band of the five auditioning today.

"Now all we can do is wait for Harry Darby to make up his mind," Sienna said as she sat next to Mark.

"Whatever the outcome, we all know we were awesome today," Mark said. "And, Tracie." He turned to her. "For someone who was so nervous, you were great up there."

Her mouth was open, but she didn't answer him. She was gawking at Aaron as he and Lily stood together in the aisle. Tracie was staring at him so hard, Mark wouldn't have been surprised if she began drooling.

"Tracie." Sienna elbowed her.

Tracie finally looked away from Aaron. "You think we'll get the gig?"

"Lily's vocals set us apart from the other bands," Mark said. "You were amazing today, Lily," he told her.

"I think Mark should be president of your fan club," George said.

"Fine with me." Lily tossed her hair. Mark loved when she did that.

Then he reminded himself to be more considerate of his girlfriend. "Sienna, you were great too. I know everyone's on edge right now, waiting for the manager to make his decision. Whether we get the gig or not, we should be proud of ourselves."

"Yeah, yeah," George said. "But I'll be a lot prouder if we get the gig."

Sienna laughed.

She was so nice, so loyal, so uncomplicated. And she was pretty, too, with skin the shade of dark maple syrup, and just as soft and sweet, and welcoming eyes and an easy smile. He had started seeing Sienna just a few months after moving to San Diego, and her constancy and warmth had eased some of the heartache that had nearly destroyed him the year before in L.A. Tracie was right about Sienna and him being the perfect couple.

Sienna caught his gaze, beamed at him, and then sat on his lap. She put her arms around his neck. "You okay, baby?"

He leaned away from her. "I just wish Darby would make up his mind already."

The manager finally stood up and faced everyone waiting at Waves. He cleared his throat, then announced, "All you bands were decent, but Amber Road was freakin' hot. I'm giving the slot to them."

The band shouted, "Yes!" and "All right!" and pumped their fists.

Aaron yelled, "Great choice!"

Yeah! Mark's heart throbbed as if it would burst out of his skin. Besides his incredible excitement, he felt a sense of victory, as well as relief—all their rehearsals and songwriting efforts and his difficult decision to make Lily lead singer had paid off. Mostly, though, he felt incredible joy.

"You guys nailed it up there today," the manager said. "You keep rocking like that, I'll be hiring you as freakin' headliners."

"Awesome!" Mark said. "Thank you."

Darby gave them a thumbs-up. "I'm penciling you in for this Thursday night and counting on you to blow this joint away and make anyone still standing want to come back for more. After your first gig, I'll decide whether to bring you back the next week. And thanks, everyone, for coming." He lumbered backstage.

Sienna slipped off Mark's lap and announced, "Hugs all around."

Tracie, George, and Lily rushed over, and soon the five band members were clutching each other tightly.

As Mark hugged Sienna, he took in her nice lavender scent and appreciated her white lacy dress that accented her smooth dark skin. "We did it! Together we did it. Thanks for always being there for me and the band," Mark said as they embraced.

He meant it. Sienna seemed to want the success of Amber Road as much as he did. Not only was she always on time for practices, she played guitar on her own five days a week. And she had organized most of the practices, sending e-mail notices and reminders to everyone. Mark knew that Sienna's hard work ever since he'd formed the band last year had helped bring Amber Road to the point they were at now.

Next, Mark hugged Lily. His arms fit around her differently than they did with Sienna. Lily was tall and willowy, while Sienna was petite and more muscular. He couldn't help noticing Lily's perfume, which smelled like a forest after a rainfall, fresh and tangy with an exotic spice to it. Because her outfit was so skimpy, hugging her meant that Mark mostly touched soft skin. Lily could take a guy's breath away. And rational thought.

Mark told himself to stop thinking with his hormones. If he treated Lily as anything other than a friend and fellow performer, not only would Sienna be hurt but the whole dynamic of the band could be destroyed. *Focus on Amber Road,* he lectured himself, *on our success, not on the female band members, not on how supple Lily feels in your arms.*

Oh, man, they'd been holding each other a long time. Was Lily hugging him a little longer and closer than the others? Or was he just fantasizing about that? Whatever it was, he didn't want to let her go.

three

"Mark," Sienna asked him while they were getting ready to leave Waves, "now that Amber Road is going places, will you finally tell us why you picked its name?"

He shook his head. "Hey, the band name works, right? It's good enough for Darby to ask us to play here on Thursday night. So don't worry about it."

"I was just wondering. Don't take my head off," Sienna said.

"Sorry." Mark smiled, but Sienna noticed that his eyes looked sad. *Who is Amber, anyway?* she wondered. An ex-girlfriend?

"It's all right," Sienna said. It really wasn't, though. She and Mark had been going out almost a year. Didn't he trust her enough by now? She couldn't imagine keeping big secrets from him. Sometimes she wondered if he loved her as much as she loved him. "We'd better take off so we can catch that movie," Sienna said.

Mark glanced around the empty club. "We're the last people left here."

"You guys are going to the movies?" Aaron asked, as if they were going to a sewage plant.

Aaron just rubbed Sienna the wrong way. "You have a problem with that?" she asked him, trying not to scowl.

"Yeah, as a matter of fact. You just won a slot at Waves. You guys need to celebrate. Lily needs to celebrate. We all do."

"We?" Mark asked.

"My sister's band rocks. I'll drink to that."

"I'll drink to anything," George said.

Tracie giggled.

"In fact, I'll buy the drinks tonight," Aaron said. "I've got a fake ID and my parents' credit card burning a hole in my pocket."

"Mr. Hot Pants, eh?" George joked.

"That's what the girls say," Aaron retorted. "The rumors about me are all true. Hear that, Tracie?"

"The only rumor I heard about you is that you're full of yourself," Tracie said, but she was blushing.

Sienna's cheeks felt warm too, mostly because she didn't like how Aaron was talking. "You guys can go drink yourselves stupid." She took a few steps toward the exit. "But Mark and I already made plans to—"

"We'll party with you," Mark interrupted. "It isn't every day our band gets its big chance."

"Or every day someone offers to buy the drinks," George said.

"I always buy drinks for pretty ladies," Aaron said. "But for the guys of Amber Road, consider this a one-shot deal."

"That's cool. Thanks," Mark said. "I'm all for having a good time, as long as no one drinks and drives."

He was so uptight about that, Sienna thought. Everyone knew that drunk drinking was bad—it had been pounded into them enough times in driver's ed—but Mark had to bring it up practically any time someone mentioned alcohol. What was that all about, anyway? Had he been caught drunk driving? Or hurt by a drunk driver? They'd been dating and playing in Amber Road for almost a year, but there was still so much about Mark that Sienna didn't know.

"The band usually just rehearses in my garage," Mark said. "Going out together to celebrate sounds like fun."

Sienna forced herself to smile, but she clenched her fists. Earlier, she and Mark had spent a half hour figuring out which movie to see tonight. She'd been looking forward to being alone with him. She accepted that Amber Road was the most important thing in Mark's life, but they'd been with the rest of the band for hours already today. Wasn't that enough for him?

"Let's go to the beach," Aaron said. "Lifeguard station seven. I'll stop off at my favorite liquor store first, and meet you there. This is turning out to be a great day." He started to walk away.

It is great, Sienna told herself. She made herself unclench her fists and tried to persuade herself to be happy. They had aced the audition, something she and Mark had been hoping for like crazy. Amber Road was important to Sienna too. Mark was obviously ecstatic, and she should be also. And they could still be together tonight, even if Aaron and the others were there too. *It's all good,* she told herself.

But she didn't like how long Mark had hugged Lily—longer than he'd hugged her, his girlfriend for God's sake. Sure, Lily's voice was a factor in the band's success. But Lily's wild attitude and striking appearance could be potent to her and Mark's relationship, Sienna sensed.

"Aaron," Tracie called after him. "Make sure you buy some good drinks for me."

Tracie's joking, right? Sienna wondered.

Aaron turned around. "Don't you worry your pretty head, babe. I'll get you something special. I'd love to see you really loosen up."

"Her name is Tracie, not *babe*," Sienna said. "And she doesn't drink alcohol." Tracie never even took a sip of beer. She and Carter had always been straight arrows.

"Aaron can call me *babe*. It's not exactly derogatory, you know," Tracie said. "And just because I never drank before doesn't mean I'm not willing to try new things."

Huh? Sienna stared at Tracie. Who was this girl? And what had she done with her best friend, Tracie?

Aaron swaggered out of the club. He seemed like the biggest lech. If Sienna weren't so excited about scoring the Waves gig, she'd probably have felt sick to her stomach.

Sienna thought she should warn Tracie about Aaron in private. Tracie was so innocent. The only guy she'd ever dated was Carter, and they hadn't even had sex. Sienna wondered if her friend had even heard of the term *player*. Because Sienna knew that's what Aaron was—a Player with a capital P. "I think we should talk, Tracie. Let's drive to the beach together," she suggested.

"Sienna, are you girls going to be the designated drivers?" Mark asked.

"I'm definitely not, for once," Tracie said.

"I'll do it tonight," Mark volunteered.

Sienna kissed his cheek. "I won't drink either, then. Since neither of us is going to drink, why don't we just stick to our original plan of seeing a movie?"

"And miss a Amber Road celebration? No way." He looked at Lily and smiled. "You're coming too, right?"

Lily tossed back her long hair. She probably practiced that move in front of her mirror. "I never miss a party if I can help it."

She might as well have just come out and said, *I'm so much more fun than your boring girlfriend,* Sienna thought.

"Lily, I can give you a ride to the beach," Mark offered. "And later tonight I can drive you home. That way you can drink whatever you want."

Oh, great, Sienna thought. *Not only are Mark and I not going to the movies, but now, while I'm trying to give Tracie a quick education in avoiding skanky guys like Aaron, Mark will be chauffeuring Lily all over town. Just great.*

"I'd love a ride," Lily said.

Of course she would, Sienna said to herself. *She'll probably suggest taking the scenic route too.*

"Lifeguard station seven, right?" Tracie said. "We'll see you there. Come on, Sienna. This is going to be fun."

"Tracie, are you sure you want to drink?" Sienna asked her.

"You drink, Sienna. You guys all do."

"We don't get straight A's either. We're not in the running for valedictorian like you and Carter are."

"Straight A's. Me and Carter. Teetotalers. That can get a little boring."

"In Europe, all the teens drink," Lily said. "Even children have wine with dinner like it's no big deal."

Europe again. Sienna had to force herself not to roll her eyes.

"Let's get to the beach." Mark headed for the exit. "Good-bye club Waves, hello ocean waves."

"Okay." Sienna followed him, but he didn't look back.

four

Sienna and Tracie got in Sienna's Miata. As soon as Tracie closed the car door, Sienna opened up to her. "I'm so tired of hearing Lily go on about Europe. It's like she thinks she's all superior to us because she lived there. And I think she's been flirting with Mark. I bet she'd have no qualms about stealing him away from me."

"Oh, Sienna, you don't know that," Tracie said.

"I don't know that, but I sure suspect it." Sienna sighed. "I've seen how they look at each other."

Tracie patted her friend's shoulder. "Mark isn't like money in a cash register. No one can steal him unless he wants to be stolen."

Tracie had a point. But on the other hand, if a sexy girl set out to steal Mark, Sienna wasn't sure he'd be strong enough to say no. Was Lily trying to take Mark from her? Was he interested?

"You've spent as much time with Mark and Lily as I have. Honestly, Tracie, have you noticed them eyeing each other?"

Tracie shook her head. "You guys are a good couple. I wouldn't stress. Lily's got nothing over you."

"Yeah, what would Mark want with a gorgeous girl with wild red hair almost to her ass, who sings like Celine Dion?"

Tracie punched Sienna lightly on the arm. "Shut up. You're a great guitarist and a good singer and gorgeous too."

Sienna was so happy to have Tracie in her life. They'd been best friends since elementary school, and were each other's sounding boards, cheerleaders, and biggest fans. She trusted Tracie completely. Hearing Tracie say she shouldn't worry about losing Mark really eased her mind.

Now that they were away from Lily and Mark and all the bands at Waves, Sienna wondered if the pressure of the audition had magnified her suspicions. And maybe an hour or so hanging at the beach was just what she needed to chill out. She could probably get Mark to go for a walk with her, take off their shoes, get their feet wet, make out in the surf. It could be very romantic. She felt a lot better already.

Sienna glanced at Tracie. "You and Carter should double-date with me and Mark tonight. After the beach, we'll still probably have time to see a movie."

"Maybe. I guess I should call and see if Carter wants to meet us on the beach."

"Don't sound so excited to talk to him," Sienna said sarcastically, and the girls laughed.

"Seriously, though," Sienna said, "I'm surprised you didn't

already call him. Don't you want to celebrate with your boy-friend? Your very nice boyfriend, I should add. I like Carter a lot. Everyone likes Carter. He's a great guy. I don't know how he does it all—student government, planning the spring dance, cap-tain of the water polo team. And you guys are a good couple."

"Uh-huh," Tracie said. She didn't exactly sound enthused. "Sienna, sometimes I almost feel like a robot, programmed to lead my life a certain way. Date a nice guy—"

"A nice, handsome, smart, water polo–captain guy."

"Yeah, I know. Carter's perfect. And so is our dream of the Ivy League. Everything's just so perfect it makes me want to scream sometimes. What if I want things to be unpredictable? Wild, even? Like Aaron Bouchet."

Sienna shook her head. "Girl, is that why you're acting so crazy? You got a thing for Aaron Bouchet?"

"You have to admit he's totally hot. The guy could be an underwear model. Not that I've ever imagined such a thing." Tracie giggled. "Not much, anyway."

This wasn't funny. "Yeah, Aaron's good-looking, I'll give you that. But you're going to throw away a nice, sweet guy like Carter for Aaron Bouchet? Is he even planning to go to college? Will he even graduate high school? What do you have in common with him except for lust?"

Tracie shrugged. "What else do we need?"

"Friendship. Shared values. Similar ambitions."

"You sound like a parent. No. A grandparent. It's not like I'm going to marry the guy."

Sienna could hardly believe she was having this conversa-tion. "I always thought you and Carter would get married. Aren't you two saving your virginities for that?"

"That was his idea." Tracie shook her head. "Honestly,

Sienna, I don't think holding off on sex even bothers Carter that much. But it's killing me. Girls have needs too."

Sienna laughed. "Tell me about it. Mark and I first made love about a month after we started dating. He keeps a blanket in his trunk just in case the urge hits us. And, honey, it hits us a lot." As she spoke, she realized she shouldn't be worried about losing Mark to Lily. They were such a good couple, and not just when they made love. They'd written some great songs together and shared the same taste in music. They had never even argued. But Carter and Tracie didn't argue, and Tracie was thinking about ditching him for Aaron. If their relationship wasn't secure, nobody's was.

Tracie said, "I hate to think that if I marry Carter like everyone expects me to, he'll be pretty much the only guy I ever make out with in my entire life. I've only kissed three guys before Carter, and two of them were during a spin-the-bottle game in eighth grade. The third guy slobbered all over me. Yuck."

"Oh, I remember that guy," Sienna said. "Daniel Moon, right? You called him The Slobster behind his back."

Tracie grinned. "He was really short and he had weird moles too."

"Well, Aaron's handsome, and I guess some girls could find him charming," Sienna said. "But can you trust him? Personally, I wouldn't touch him with a ten-foot pole. And I bet Aaron sticks his pole in a lot of places, if you know what I mean."

"He seems like a nice guy to me," Tracie said.

Sienna doubted she could change Tracie's mind about him. But at least she could try to get help. "Hey, hurry up and call Carter. We can swing by and pick him up. He lives right on our way, doesn't he?" Sienna said.

"Not really." Tracie shook her head.

"Close enough," Sienna said.

Tracie groaned, but pulled out her cell phone and called Carter. She was in the middle of telling him they got the club gig and asking if he wanted to hit the beach when Sienna thought of something.

"Ask him if he has any wood for a fire," Sienna interrupted her friend. She didn't trust Aaron in the dark. Or Lily either, for that matter.

After Tracie hung up the phone and said that Carter had agreed to go to the beach, Sienna felt better. She told herself to relax. She'd probably have a great time tonight celebrating with her friends.

Fortunately, once they picked up Carter, everything seemed to be back to normal. Carter put a big armful of wood in Sienna's trunk, kissed Tracie, thanked Sienna for the ride, and congratulated both of them for their winning audition. He was such a terrific guy. Sienna knew there was no way Tracie would blow him off for Aaron. She was so glad he could make it. *Maybe,* Sienna said to herself, *I'll end up having a better time on the beach with the band than I would staring at a movie screen with Mark.*

By the time they arrived, the other band members and Aaron were already getting settled. George and Aaron and a skinny Asian girl were carrying bags of beer from Aaron's Porsche. Was the girl Aaron's date? Sienna hoped so, so she could stop worrying about Tracie. But knowing George's long history of girlfriends, Sienna suspected the girl had come with him. She could even be George's sister or cousin. Except they looked nothing alike. Despite both of them being Asian, George had a long black ponytail and a pudgy body, while the girl was short-haired and thin.

Mark stood on the sand, very close to Lily. Sienna rushed to him and held his hand. If she had to grasp hold of his hand all night to keep Lily's claws off him, she would.

Aaron, George, and the Asian girl met up with the others and set down the bags of beer on the sand. George introduced the girl as Midori. "She doesn't speak any English, but we totally connect with our eyes and our smiles." He put his arm around her and they looked into each other's eyes and smiled, as if to prove George's point.

Carter smiled too, and put his arm around Tracie, who gave him a weak smile in return. "Thanks for bringing the wood," she said. "Why don't you start the fire now? Your arms must be killing you after carrying all that stuff."

Was she trying to get Carter out of the way?

As soon as he left for the fire pit, Aaron announced to the rest of the group, "I hope you're in the mood for drinking."

"Hell, yeah," Lily said.

Aaron pointed to the brown bags by his feet. "I got Heineken, Corona, and Pageant Ale, which is British."

"Guys, did you happen to bring soda or water for Tracie and Carter?" Sienna asked. "They don't drink alcohol."

"But as of now I drink. What do you think would be good to lose my virginity with?" Tracie giggled. "My beer virginity, I mean."

"Tracie, are you sure you want to do this?" Carter called from the fire pit. "It's totally illegal."

"It's also totally fun," Lily said.

"I want to live a little, okay?" Tracie said.

Carter walked over. "I don't think it's okay."

"I wasn't asking you." She sounded snide, not like the sweet person Sienna thought she knew so well. "You're on the debate team, Carter. You should know what a rhetorical question is."

To Sienna's relief, Carter held his ground. "I don't want to debate you, Tracie. I'd probably end up sounding like a blabbering idiot against you, anyway."

The guy was so modest, Sienna thought.

"I'm sorry for getting all worked up," Tracie said. "I've been stressed all day about the audition."

"I wish I'd been there," Carter said. "I bet you were awesome. I just want to make sure you know what you're getting into. I mean, you're not only underage, but it's illegal for anyone to have alcohol on the beach. An arrest could make Yale revoke your acceptance. I don't want to go to Yale without you, Tracie." He put his arm around her again. "I'm counting on you to keep me warm during those horrible Connecticut winters, not to mention proofread my English papers."

Sienna added her own admonition. "A lot of people don't drink. Tracie, you shouldn't feel like you have to do it to fit in."

"Please just bring me a can of beer already, or I'll get it myself," Tracie said.

Sienna sighed. She and Carter couldn't exactly kidnap Tracie and force her away from the alcohol, and Aaron. At least they'd warned her. "Looks like Carter already started a little fire. Let's all move over to the fire pit," she suggested, thinking that she could at least keep Tracie nearby and out of the dark.

The group walked over to the fire. Aaron gave Tracie a Heineken on the way. "This is probably best for virgins." He smirked. "Beer virgins, I mean."

"I can't remember back that far," Lily joked.

Tracie opened the can and took a sip. She made a face as if the beer had come from the toilet.

George laughed. Next to him, Midori laughed too.

"It's an acquired taste," he said. Midori nodded.

"Tracie, you don't have to drink the rest," Carter said.

"Take a chill pill." She had another sip and made the same face. Then she took a long swig. She still looked disgusted, though she didn't have quite the toilet-water expression she wore a minute ago.

"I like a girl who can handle her liquor," Aaron said. "I like a girl who can't handle her liquor even better."

What a sketch bag.

And what a sketch Lily was for laughing at Aaron's joke.

Carter said, "Look, Aaron—"

"I can handle anything." Tracie gulped down more beer.

"You sure knew how to handle the guitar tonight," George said. Midori nodded again.

"I like a girl with fast hands," Aaron said.

Total sketch. Ick.

Carter moved toward Aaron. "Stay away from my girlfriend," he growled. Sienna had never heard him sound so angry before.

"Dudes, come on." George stepped between them while Midori nodded. George wasn't exactly a physical threat. He was average height and out of shape. But he used humor as a distraction tool, or as an *attraction* tool when he was anywhere near a pretty girl. "I brought over a surprise," he said. He opened a grocery bag on the sand and pulled out a stack of Barney birthday party hats. "Put these on, dudes, and let's really party." He set one on his own head and then passed them around. Mark and the girls started laughing, and Aaron and Carter put down their fists. Everyone almost doubled over when George sang, off-key, "If all the raindrops were lemon drops and gumdrops, oh what a rain it would be."

Mark called out, "We should add that song to our set list! Maybe do 'If You're Happy and You Know It' too."

"Let's quit the nightclub scene and do children's birthday parties instead," Sienna joked. Everyone had calmed down, most importantly Aaron and Carter.

George said, "Anyone remember this song? I'll give you a hint. Barney sang it at the end of the show." He sang, "I love you, you love me, we're a happy family."

Soon everyone was joining in, even Midori with a thick Japanese accent, and laughing.

Sienna gave George's ponytail a playful yank. "You're the best."

"I know, man. That's what all the girls tell me."

Midori nodded.

"In my dreams, anyway."

Midori nodded again.

"Hey, what's a Barney party without cold beer? I hope you bought a lot of Corona," George told Aaron.

He threw a can to George, who in less than a minute caught it, opened it, and chugged half of it down.

Soon everyone but Mark, Carter, and Sienna were drinking. "Drink if you think Amber Road is going places!" George shouted.

They drank.

"Drink if you think Mark and Lily and Sienna could all be finalists on *American Idol*," George yelled, so they drank to that too.

Sienna noted that Tracie finished her beer and got another. Maybe she would drink herself sick and throw up and turn off Aaron and never want to drink again. Sienna could only hope.

"Drink if you think Tracie is the hottest guitarist on the planet," Aaron said.

"Watch it," Carter warned.

"Carter, you weren't there today so you wouldn't know," Tracie said. "I was pretty darn hot tonight, if I do say so myself." She took a big swig of her Heineken. "I think I'm getting used to the beer taste."

"I've got plenty more for you," Aaron said.

"She's had enough." Carter put his arm around her.

"You're not driving, are you, Tracie? I can take you home," Aaron offered.

"No, you can't take her home," Carter said.

"Guys," Mark said. "We just had the best performance ever. Let's focus on that."

"Actually, let's just focus on me," George said. Midori nodded again.

Everyone laughed except Carter. His hands were clenched.

Sienna wished he'd punch Aaron in his fat mouth and get Tracie off the beach and away from the beer and the Bouchets. *Carter's only flaw*, Sienna thought, *is that he's too nice*. Tracie apparently needed someone meaner, who would yell at her to stop acting like an idiot and tolerating jerks like Aaron.

"When I'm a world-famous drummer, you guys can say you helped me get my start. And I'll pretend I don't remember you," George joked.

Midori nodded.

"Hey, we'll all be famous together," Mark said. "One for all and all for one, or however that expression goes."

"Hear, hear," Sienna said, remembering how Lily had bragged earlier today that Harry Darby would pick her for the gig, as if the rest of Amber Road were at Waves just as background.

"I've always wanted to be a rock star," George said. "Mostly so I can act like a spoiled brat and be surrounded by bodyguards and gorgeous groupies, and demand cases of Evian and exactly thirty-four blueberries arranged on a glass plate in a perfect isosceles triangle in my dressing room."

Midori nodded again, but everyone else laughed.

"Is that really your dream?" Tracie asked George.

"Well, my real dream job is to be a trash collector or a busboy."

The group laughed again.

"But I may have to settle for my third-place secret desire to be a rock 'n' roll superstar. I hate to leave, but Midori and I have an exciting adventure ahead of us tonight," George said.

Midori nodded.

"I'm not sure what that adventure will be, but I think Midori will nod again."

She nodded.

"George!" Sienna scolded.

He shrugged. "I'm just kidding." He waved good-bye, took Midori's hand, and made his way with her to his motorcycle.

"Maybe we really will be a success," Mark said. "And we'll all be rock 'n' roll superstars."

"I just want to make good music and have the chance to perform in front of audiences," Sienna said. "I don't really care about being rich and famous. My true secret desire would be to travel around the country touring with Mark and the rest of the band. That would be so cool."

"You know what my secret desire is?" Lily asked.

"To find out that you were adopted and therefore don't share any of Aaron's genes?" Carter said.

"Ha ha." She shook her head. "I'd like to pose naked for a great sculptor and have my body immortalized for, like, thousands of years."

"What a coincidence," Mark said. "My secret desire is to become a great sculptor and sculpt Lily when she's naked."

"Ooh, I love it," Lily said.

"I bet you do." Sienna glared at Lily, then Mark. How dare they flirt with each other right in front of her! "So much for my secret desire of traveling around with the band. Mark and Lily would probably leave me in the middle of a desert in Arizona or something with no food or water."

"Sorry, Sienna." Mark shrugged. "You know I was just kidding."

Was he? She wasn't so sure of that.

"Carter, how about you?" Mark asked. "I bet you want to do something important and good."

"Why not? It beats doing something trivial and bad," Carter said. "I'd like to be a senator representing the state of California."

Aaron sneered. "How important and superior you are, Carter." He turned to Tracie. "So what's your secret desire? To be a senator's wife?"

Carter pulled Tracie closer to him. "She wants to be a public-interest attorney with training in forensics so she can save innocent people from death row."

"Oh, Carter. That's just what I told the college interviewer." Tracie moved away from her boyfriend, stumbling a bit. "You want to hear my real secret desire?"

"Yeah, babe." Aaron licked his lips.

"Don't say anything you'll regret," Sienna said, worried that Tracie's secret desire was named Aaron.

"I never get to say anything I'll regret. Or *do* anything I'll regret. It's no fun."

"Well, why do it if you'll just regret it later?" Carter asked.

"That's exactly why my secret desire has nothing to do with you, Carter."

"Maybe you should keep it secret then," Sienna tried again.

"God, Sienna, you're such a busybody," Tracie said.

Sienna told herself that was just the alcohol talking. Still, she couldn't help feeling angry that her best friend was calling her names. She was just trying to stop her from embarrassing herself.

Tracie cleared her throat. "My secret desire is to hook up with Aaron for a night."

Sienna shook her head. Just as she'd suspected. Beer could made people so stupid.

Carter dropped the arm he had around Tracie and stepped to the side as if she repulsed him. The rest of Amber Road didn't respond to what Tracie had just said. It was as if they had frozen from shock.

Aaron sure responded, though. "Awesome, Tracie!" he exclaimed. "But you'll want to spend more than one night with me. More like a lifetime."

Carter crossed his arms. "You two are making me sick!"

"Oh my God, I have, like, the greatest idea," Lily said.

"Put a muzzle on Aaron?" Carter asked.

"Ha ha. No." She looked at Mark as she spoke. "It's really a great idea. Just for fun."

Sienna had a feeling this great idea of Lily's would be no fun for her.

"Tell us," Mark said, staring right back at Lily, almost as if they were the only people on the beach.

"Promise you won't get all uptight?"

"Me? No way." Mark's gaze remained on Lily.

"Okay. Why don't we—" She paused for a smile. Her eyes glinted, *evilly*, Sienna thought. "Why don't we trade boy-friends and girlfriends?"

"What?" Sienna couldn't help exclaiming. She knew it. Lily was dying to get hold of Mark, any way she could. At least her scheming was out in the open now.

"It would just be, like, for fun," Lily said.

How was that fun? Sienna had to put a stop to it. She tried to stand tall, though she felt like she could barely stand at all. "You've got to be kidding," she told Lily.

But Lily didn't laugh. Neither did anyone else.

five

"I'm totally serious about trading boyfriends," Lily said.

And Tracie was totally embarrassed. She had blurted out that fantasy about hooking up with Aaron just because she was feeling so impulsive tonight. It was mostly the beer talking, she knew. She didn't think anyone would actually try to help her fantasy come true. Who did Lily think she was? The Make-A-Wish Foundation? Tracie smiled at that, and also because she was buzzed.

"I can tell Tracie wants to trade guys," Lily said. "Look at that smile on her face."

Oh, God. Now she was even more embarrassed. She dropped her smile.

"Swapping boyfriends would just be for fun. It's not like we'd be getting married or anything," Lily said.

Why wasn't anyone objecting? Tracie looked around. Mark

stood frozen, his mouth open a little. Carter had his arms crossed over his chest. Sienna was shaking her head. Aaron and Lily were the only people who seemed happy. Aaron's lips were turned up so high, she didn't think his grin could get any bigger if *Sports Illustrated* photographers were shooting the swimsuit edition on the beach and asked him to pose with the supermodels.

Seeing his smile brought back Tracie's. She had to admit that despite being attached to Carter, she'd been crushing on Aaron since she first saw him wandering the hallway with a map of their school a few months ago. She had offered to walk him to his class, and it wasn't just from the goodness of her heart. Actually, it was from the badness of her heart. Now here he was, grinning over the prospect of hooking up with her, a prospect suggested by his own twin sister. Maybe while she had been fantasizing about Aaron the last few months, he had done the same about her. She couldn't have stopped smiling even if she'd wanted to. Lily's suggestion to swap guys might be the greatest idea anyone from Amber Road had come up with since Mark had thought to audition at Waves.

"I'll take Mark," Lily said.

Oh, no. Tracie looked at her best friend. Sienna's jaw was clenched, her eyebrows furrowed.

"I want Tracie," Aaron said.

Tracie's thoughts left Sienna as soon as she heard Aaron's voice. She loved that it was rich and smooth and full of confidence.

"I want Tracie right now, tonight," he said.

Whoa. Tracie felt tingly. Aaron sounded so sexy. He looked so sexy. He probably tasted sexy too. She wanted him right now, tonight, too. Except she couldn't look at him. She was probably blushing like crazy and smiling like a goofball. She couldn't look at Carter either. He must feel so hurt. Thinking of him now made Tracie lose that tingly feeling.

"That leaves Sienna and Carter," Lily said. She sounded so official, as if she were at a business meeting.

"Me and Carter?" Sienna asked as if the idea were gross.

It *was* sort of gross, Tracie thought. Her best friend hooking up with her boyfriend. What if Sienna and Carter made out tonight? Tracie's stomach churned like a mixer on low speed, and she didn't think it was just from the beer.

"Let's do it," Aaron said in that blustery voice of his.

Again, Tracie's thoughts turned away from everything except Aaron. "Let's do it," she said with a newfound confidence and sultriness in her voice. She was fully aware of the double entendre, and played up to it. "Let's do it right now," she said.

six

"Game *on*, Tracie," Aaron said. "Let's get moving, babe."

"Tracie, don't," Carter said. "You don't know what you're doing. You're drunk."

Tracie just stood there, next to Carter but staring into the fire pit, not sure what to do. She knew what she wanted to do—run off with Aaron. But what *should* she do? Stay with her good, solid boyfriend and maybe wonder for the rest of her life what would have happened if she had left with Aaron tonight? Or embrace Lily's boyfriend swap, and Aaron, and possibly ruin her three-year relationship with Carter along with the respect of her friends?

Aaron walked over to her and took her hand. Tracie liked a guy who took charge. Especially a guy with shiny large eyes and thick, luscious hair that begged to be played with. He led her away from the group and she didn't object.

Maybe she would have changed her mind if Carter had protested more, grabbed her back, threatened to kick Aaron's ass. But he did nothing apart from asking her to stay. And that was an example of what had bothered Tracie about Carter lately. He was so concerned with doing the right thing, being nice to teachers so they'd write good college references, going to every debate practice or student government meeting even if it was a beautiful day and his girlfriend would rather take a walk on the beach or fool around at the park. He never drank or had sex or even broke curfew. And tonight, he wouldn't fight Aaron for her. So Tracie squeezed Aaron's hand and whispered, "Let's go."

"Are you all right to drive?" Mark called after them.

"I only had one beer," Aaron said.

"Well, drive carefully."

"In a red Porsche convertible?" Aaron said. "No way. That thing's made for driving like a maniac."

"Don't you dare!" Mark yelled.

"Chill. I was joking. I've got precious cargo to deliver. And we're going to have the best night of our lives." Aaron pinched Tracie's bottom.

She giggled. Aaron did just what he wanted, regardless of who was watching or what people might think. He might be arrogant, but he was a welcome change from conservative Carter.

"Tracie!" Carter yelled after her.

She stopped and turned around. Carter stayed where he was, his arms crossed. Maybe if he were more forceful, she'd walk away from Aaron.

But he wasn't. "Don't do it," he pleaded as he stood on the beach.

"Don't worry, Carter. It's just for fun, remember?" She was slurring her words.

Aaron moved forward, pulling her along. She didn't resist, and walked close to him.

On the way to his car, he whistled as if taking her away from her boyfriend was no big deal to a smooth guy like him. Next to him, her hand in his, she felt totally secure. He was so tall and so muscular. Carter was strong too, but in a lanky, quick way. Aaron seemed much more rugged and masculine.

Tracie tried to make out the tune Aaron was whistling. It sounded like a cheerful one, whatever it was. Her mind wasn't working one hundred percent. *Shoot, it's not even working seventy-five percent,* she said to herself right before stumbling and falling on the sand. Her body wasn't working so well either. She felt slow and clumsy, but happy.

After he helped her up, Aaron put his arm around her.

Very, very happy. Tracie leaned into him. She liked touching his hard stomach, plus she needed assistance holding herself up.

Aaron stopped whistling once they got to his Porsche. He opened the car door for her and helped her in, kissing her lightly on the lips as soon as she was seated.

Even that little kiss made Tracie flush. She didn't know if it was the alcohol or Aaron, but she felt more turned on now than she had during last week's heavy makeout session with Carter.

Carter. He was probably so upset. What in the world was she doing? He might never forgive her for tonight. It was stupid of her to blurt out her fantasy about Aaron, and more stupid to agree to this boyfriend swap, and probably stupidest of all to be going off with Aaron to who knew where. Tomorrow morning, when she was sober and likely hung over, she'd probably hate herself for all the stupid things she did tonight.

But that was tomorrow. Right now, she was incredibly happy.

Aaron sauntered around the car to the driver's side, got in, and closed the door.

The car was warm and smelled like leather. She moved her face close to Aaron and sniffed. He still smelled like the salty beach air.

"So you've been crushing on me, huh?" Aaron said as he pulled out of the parking lot.

"A little." Tracie looked away, embarrassed.

"Just a little?"

"A lot." *Oh, God,* she chastised herself. *Why am I telling Aaron this when I have a boyfriend?*

"Did you know that I've always thought, from the second I first saw you at school, that you were gorgeous?" He put his right hand on her cheek, turning her face toward him.

God, he looked good. He felt good.

He stroked her neck, then let his hand slip over the top of her chest and rest there. "I can't wait to get you to my house," he said.

"Your house? Oh, no. We shouldn't. I can't . . ."

"You're a virgin, right?" His hand moved back to her cheek. "I didn't mean tonight, not necessarily, anyway. Hey, babe, I'll wait for you. Let's go somewhere fun. You ever play pool before?"

"Swimming?"

Aaron laughed.

"Oh, wait, pool. Like, with a stick." She giggled. For an honor student, she sure could be dim sometimes. Of course, she'd also just drunk two cans of beer. "I'm a little buzzed," she explained. "I'm not exactly a pool shark, but I used to play eight ball at my cousin Benji's house. He moved a few years ago."

"I know this great pool hall in Mission Valley. It's kind of a dive, but most are, right?"

"Right." Tracie had never been to a pool hall before, but she wanted to be with Aaron and she didn't want to go to his house.

"You ever played at a pool hall before?"

"To tell the truth, no. But it sounds like fun," Tracie said.

"A pool hall virgin too. You know, there's a first time for everything." Aaron stroked her neck before returning his hand to the steering wheel.

Tracie felt guilty—a little, anyway. If Carter ever found out Aaron was touching her like this, he'd really be upset. But this adventure was just the type of thing she'd been craving lately. Studying with Carter or going on their Saturday night movie dates had gotten old, especially because they'd been together for years.

Aaron drove his Porsche into the lot of a dark strip mall, then parked in front of a building with neon letters that read "Jack's Poo Hall."

"Poo Hall?" Tracie said. "You're taking me to a poo hall?" She burst out laughing and pointed to the damaged sign.

Aaron laughed with her, and Tracie thought that just for this moment alone—sitting in the leather seat of a red sports car, next to a gorgeous guy who was giving her an experience she'd never have gotten with Carter—all the chances she'd taken tonight were worth it.

Aaron got out of the car. He didn't walk around and open the door for her, like Carter always did. But Tracie decided that was an outmoded tradition anyway. She was certainly capable of opening a car door.

She had a little difficulty walking. Actually, she wasn't standing perfectly either. Aaron put his strong arm around her and she leaned her body into him as they headed into Jack's.

Tracie had pictured pool halls as dank places full of biker gangs who smoked and cursed and made risky bets. But it wasn't like that at all. For one thing, smoking wasn't allowed in California businesses anymore, so the old movies showing murky interiors were misleading. And although a few guys looked grungy and angry, plenty of them appeared clean-cut. There were some girls inside too.

Aaron set up the balls on the pool table while Tracie practiced holding the cue stick. Her first try was a scratch, especially embarrassing because Aaron got three balls in the pockets on his turn.

He helped her shoot next time, standing behind her with his hand over hers and their bodies almost inseparable. Now he smelled less like the salty ocean air and more like a musky cologne or aftershave. She didn't knock any balls in, but at least she didn't scratch this time. And, really, who cared? She just liked the feel of Aaron's body so close behind her.

On Aaron's next turn, he pocketed two balls. He said he used to play in London and claimed he was excellent at darts, too, which was popular in the pub he had frequented. Tracie had never even been out of the United States except to go to Tijuana for the day. He was so exotic.

On her third turn, when she finally got a ball in the pocket, Aaron shouted, "All right!" and Tracie threw her arms around him and tried to kiss his cheek. He turned his head and she ended up kissing his mouth. Afterward, they remained in each other's arms, laughing and hugging. They played only one game. Aaron offered to buy her another beer, but she turned him down. It had been a long day, with the audition, the beer, the crazy boyfriend trade, and the pool hall date. Tracie wouldn't have missed any of it for the world.

They got in his Porsche, but Aaron didn't turn on the ignition right away. Instead, he asked if she wanted to go to this spot in the hills of Tierrasanta where they could watch the San Diego city lights. Tracie knew what Aaron meant. *He might as well have asked me if I want to make out,* she said to herself.

She did want to. She was dying to, in fact. But she had a boyfriend to whom she'd been faithful for the entire three years they'd been together. And she wasn't sure what this guy-trading game meant exactly. Were they supposed to trade guys to talk to? To shoot pool with for one evening? Or could she make out with Aaron as much as she wanted?

"Is it okay, gorgeous, if we go by the scenic point?" Aaron asked her. "Or should I just drive you home?"

God, she liked being called gorgeous. When was the last time Carter had called her gorgeous? She couldn't even remember. Tonight was her chance to explore other guys, maybe her last chance ever, for the rest of her life. "I'd love to stop and see the view," she told Aaron.

He put his hand on her thigh. "Awesome, Tracie." He started the car.

So they were going to do more than look at city lights. The question was how much more? And how much would she be able to resist him?

seven

They had been parked for only about thirty seconds before Aaron moved his seat back as far as it would go and said, "Come here, gorgeous Tracie," and pointed to his lap.

He was so suave. When Carter took her to "look at the view," he usually made small talk for a few minutes first, as if making out with her weren't very important. She climbed over the gearshift and sat on Aaron's lap.

"Turn around, silly," he murmured. So she did, straddling him, and it was obvious he was very happy to have her there.

They kissed, a slow, openmouthed, perfect, passionate kiss. He put his arms around her, and then they were on her chest, and his fingers were inside her bra, and she pressed into him. She hadn't looked at a single city light, and she didn't care. She couldn't remember the last time Carter had made her feel like this, hot and sexy and crazy too.

Carter. Oh, God. Carter. She and Aaron had to slow down. She had a boyfriend. She was a virgin. She hardly knew Aaron at all. She closed her lips and moved her face back. "I think we need to stop," she said.

He kept his hands on her chest. "Come on, Tracie. You're making me insane." His voice was so sweet, almost pitiable.

Her cell phone rang.

"Don't answer that," Aaron said.

"It could be my parents. I don't want to worry them." She reached over and took her phone out of her purse. Aaron's hands remained on her, making it very hard to concentrate on anything but how good he made her feel. She managed to check the Caller ID. Carter.

She was too ashamed to talk to him on the phone right now. She knew that she shouldn't have messed around with Aaron. She may have been getting a little tired of her relationship with her boyfriend, but was that any excuse to cheat on him? Carter was a nice guy, loyal and honest, someone who always wanted the best for her.

She couldn't allow herself to go any further with Aaron, no matter how amazing he made her feel. That was shameful too. She turned off her phone. Then she put her hands on Aaron's arms and said, "Things are going too fast tonight. I had the best time, and I think you're a great guy, but . . ."

As she spoke, his fingers were doing incredible things inside her bra.

"Aaron. Take me home. Please." Inside, she shouted *Don't take me home! Take me! Take me here*. But she had to do the right thing.

He let go of her, kissed her cheek, even put her bra straps back on her shoulder. "Anything you want, gorgeous."

"I do want you, Aaron." The sultriness appeared in her voice again. "But not tonight, okay? Not yet," she couldn't help adding, knowing that the word *yet* could give him hope for the future.

"I understand. But what am I going to do about this?" He looked down at his pants.

They were absolutely bulging.

Tracie forced her gaze up to Aaron's face. "Poor Aaron. I'm sorry."

"You drive me completely crazy. Promise you'll go out with me again. Soon."

This was supposed to be a one-night thing, just a fun game. She had a great boyfriend.

"Please, Tracie?" He cocked his head. He looked so sweet.

This had been one of the best nights of her life. How could she turn down another one? And it wasn't fair to tease Aaron like this—making out with him, and then just as both of them were all hot, demanding that they leave. That's what she told herself, anyway. The truth was, she'd do practically anything to be with him again. And Carter didn't need to know this wouldn't be her last date with Aaron. *What you don't know won't hurt you,* she told herself. She told Aaron, "I promise we can go out again."

"Soon, Tracie. As soon as possible." He pulled her to him again and gave her one more slow, luscious kiss.

Afterward, she said again, "I promise."

eight

Lily squeezed between Sienna and Mark at the fire pit. "This is going to be, like, wild."

"It better not be," Sienna said.

But she had never before seen Mark's eyes so wide and so bright. In fact, he usually looked at her with veiled, distant eyes. Before, she'd assumed Mark's thoughts involved Amber Road or Amber herself, the mystery girl he'd named the band after. But now Sienna wondered if all this time he'd really been thinking about Lily. Ick.

Sienna didn't know whether he would even come back to her tomorrow, or ever. She bit her lip so hard she tasted blood. How could Mark risk throwing away their yearlong relationship just to fool around with Lily?

Then Sienna recalled how Mark had been looking at Lily

recently, with high frequency and high interest. And she couldn't compete with a tall redhead who went around jiggling her chest and vibrating her hips. *I might be a nice girl,* Sienna thought, *but Lily is a bad girl.* Lily had been all over the world, and probably been with guys all over the world. She was gorgeous, dangerous, and wild. Sienna supposed she could understand Mark's curiosity.

She could understand it, but she sure didn't like it. She knew Lily had suggested the swap just to get her claws on Mark. And she hated the thought of Mark picking Lily over her. But if she had said no to Lily's proposal, Mark might have hooked up with Lily anyway, and Sienna would have seemed like a prude. After Mark got to know Lily better, and saw her shallow, manipulative personality, he'd beg to have Sienna back. Maybe, possibly, hopefully.

Maybe if she acted excited about hooking up with Carter, Mark would get jealous and change his mind. She turned to Carter, whose forehead was crinkled and jaw was thrust out as if he were getting ready to step into a boxing ring. It was very apparent that he had no interest in spending time with her tonight.

She felt tears welling. She blinked them away. She wouldn't let Mark see her cry. "Let's go, Carter," she said, and took his arm and led him away as if he were an invalid or a child.

"Have fun!" Lily shouted. If she suspected that her horrible boyfriend swap plan had just broken two hearts, she sure didn't show it.

Sienna linked her arm with Carter's, and they walked in complete silence to her Miata. Sienna forced herself not to turn her head, though she was dying to see what Mark and Lily were doing together. She and Carter kept their silence while getting in the car. The noise of the doors slamming shut was jolting.

She felt like leaning against Carter and sobbing. But that would just let Lily win. She didn't want Lily or Mark ever finding out how upset she was right now. If she and Carter went somewhere tonight, Mark and Lily might think they had a good time. Maybe Mark would get jealous after all. "So where are we headed?" she asked Carter, trying to sound chipper instead of bitter, but not doing a good job of it.

"I thought we'd just drive home," he mumbled.

"Let's go out. That's the whole idea of this swap." They had to go somewhere that seemed fun just so they could report back that their date had gone great. "You know, Mark and I had talked about seeing that new horror movie tonight," she told Carter. "You want to watch that with me?"

"Not really," Carter said. "Plus, Mark will probably want to watch the movie with you. This boyfriend trade is just temporary, right?"

"Right." It had better be, anyway. "We could go over to the theater and look for something we both want to see."

"Maybe we'll run into . . ." Carter trailed off, but Sienna realized what he was going to say: Mark and Lily. Yes, of course! Mark had really wanted to see the movie, and he might decide to go with Lily. Once he saw Sienna at the multiplex with Carter, he'd get jealous, say he'd made a mistake, and spend the rest of the evening with Sienna. It was a possibility, anyway. "Let's go to the theater right now," Sienna said. "It's the one by Hotel Circle in Mission Valley."

They barely spoke on the way over, except for Carter letting out a long sigh at one point, Sienna asking him if he was okay, and him saying, "I guess," before sighing again.

How could Tracie have done this to him? Carter was such a nice guy. Plus, he was really smart and athletic and cute. *Maybe Carter and I should make out or something, just for revenge,* Sienna thought.

No, she told herself. *Why stoop to Lily and Aaron's level?* Besides, Tracie was Sienna's best friend. It was wrong to make out with Tracie's boyfriend, no matter what ridiculous game they were playing tonight. Anyway, Sienna didn't think she could make out with anyone but Mark. He was the only guy she cared about.

She parked her Miata in the theater parking lot. Carter rushed out of the passenger side and opened her car door for her. What a gentleman.

They walked through the parking lot, still without talking. Sienna looked for Mark's car, but it was hard to see much of anything in the large, dark lot. Besides, she and Carter had left while Mark and Lily were still on the beach. They couldn't have gotten here yet even if they had decided to see a movie. Sienna reminded herself she was supposed to have fun with Carter, or at least a semblance of fun. "What kind of movies do you like?" she asked him.

"Lately I've been getting into smaller films. You know, documentaries, foreign films, indies. Tracie and I go to this little theater . . . Oh, I shouldn't be talking about Tracie." His voice sounded so sad.

Sienna ignored the mention of Tracie. "I doubt we'll find anything but big Hollywood movies at this theater. Let's get in the ticket line and figure out what movie to see as we wait." They stood in line and Sienna pointed to the marquee. "You like Adam Sandler? He's in that new one—"

"Can't stand him," Carter said.

"Oh."

"How about that war movie?" Carter suggested.

"I saw it with Mark last week."

"Oh."

"David Spade is funny," Sienna said.

"On what planet?"

"Oh."

"I guess the only one left is the horror movie," Carter said. "You want to see it?"

Sienna shrugged. "I guess."

The horror movie sold out right before their turn to purchase tickets.

"Let's just go home," Carter said.

"Wait. There's got to be something else we can do. I know. The bar at the Mission Valley Inn supposedly doesn't card."

"I don't drink," Carter said. "But if you want to drown your sorrows, I'll go with you and have a soda or something."

"Thanks," Sienna said. "But let's not talk about sorrows, okay? We're supposed to be having fun."

Except that she was miserable. And Carter wasn't helping her mood any. On the drive over to the bar, he said, "I'm sorry for being rude, but I have to call Tracie. It's not just that I want her back, though I really, really do. I'm worried about her with Aaron. The guy seems like a complete jerk. What if she needs my help?"

Sienna sighed. She was dying to call Mark, but she knew it would sound too needy. "Go ahead and call Tracie. I'll try not to listen. Or I could stop the car so you can get out and talk in private."

That, apparently, was all he needed to hear. He hurriedly took the phone from his pocket and speed-dialed it.

"I hope things turn out okay," Sienna said.

"Thanks. Me too. With you and Mark, I mean." He sat next to her in the car with the phone at his ear. "She's not picking up," he said. He clicked off the phone and redialed, then held it to his ear for a long time again. Finally, he turned it off and returned it to his pocket.

"I'm sorry," Sienna said.

"It's not your fault. But just thinking about what Tracie might be doing with Aaron right now is making me sick."

"Maybe he just drove her home and she went to sleep," Sienna tried to reassure him. "Tracie's so smart. She must realize what a jerk he is." Sienna didn't really believe that, but she hoped Carter might. He must have felt awful about tonight. Sienna sure did, and she and Mark had been going out for a lot less time than Carter and Tracie.

"There's the Mission Valley Inn," Carter said flatly.

Sienna parked in its lot. "This really could be fun." She spiked her voice with false enthusiasm. "I heard if you act confident, supposedly they'll let you right into the bar. Some guys from one of the other bands at the audition told me about it today."

"Do you think Tracie's mad at me for not going to her audition today?" Carter asked.

"You had debate practice. She understood." Sienna didn't mention that Tracie and Aaron had been flirting with each other at Waves. Why upset Carter even more?

Before they could even get near the door of the bar, a bouncer stopped them and asked them for ID. When Sienna said they'd left it at home, the bouncer actually laughed and told them to come back in three years when they were old enough.

"In three years, we'll be going to classier bars than this," Carter said.

They shuffled back to the car. Carter muttered, "Four years, actually. Maybe we should feel flattered that the bouncer thought we were a year older than we really are. Or maybe the guy can't do math. Probably not a big requirement for a career as a bouncer."

Sienna smiled for a moment. "I guess it was a little ridiculous to expect them to let two seventeen-year-olds into their bar without ID."

"I can't believe Tracie drank tonight," Carter said. "What's gotten into her? Do you think she's wasted by now? She was looking pretty tipsy when we left her at the beach."

Sienna shrugged. "I don't know about Tracie, but we're supposed to be having fun."

"Yeah. Good times." Carter sighed. "A sold-out movie, a bar we can't get into, and a girl I can't stop thinking about."

"Let's get something to eat," Sienna suggested. "Nothing can go too wrong at a restaurant. You like Mexican?"

"Love it. Finally, something we agree on. How about Marco's?"

She had never been there. The name *Marco* reminded Sienna of *Mark*. But she didn't want to make things any worse than they were. So she said, "Great!" and they were on their way.

But things went wrong at the restaurant too. She got lost on the way over. The chips and salsa came almost as soon as they sat down and burned their mouths while they waited forever to get water.

Their waitress was a small, pale blond girl. "Who does she remind you of?" Carter whispered to Sienna.

Tracie, of course. The waitress wasn't as pretty, but her hair was blond and straight like Tracie's and she had a similar petite figure. "She doesn't remind me of anyone," Sienna said. "Because we're supposed to be having fun."

"Oh, yeah. Fun. Note to self." Carter pretended to write on the white tablecloth. "Have a ball, Carter. Become ecstatic."

Sienna couldn't help smiling. People always said George was funny, but Carter had a great sense of humor too.

The waitress looked at her watch. "You know, you're not my only table."

How rude! Sienna thought.

"We're not a table. We're people," Carter said. "We're your customers, your *tipping* customers, depending on how you treat us." He looked at Sienna. "Is the lady ready to order, or would she like another minute?"

"When you say it that way, I'm happy to order now," Sienna said.

Once they'd given the surly waitress their orders, they sat silently until Sienna thought of a conversation starter that didn't involve Mark or Tracie. "So, is student council keeping you busy?" she asked.

"Very. The spring dance is only a few weeks away and— Oh, no. You think Tracie will still be my date for it? What if she wants to go with Aaron instead?"

"Carter. Please stop talking about Tracie. You're supposed to be hooking up with me, not using me as your therapist."

"Sorry, Sienna. I'm usually better company. It's just that—"

Just then, the Tracie-look-alike waitress came by with their food. When she tried to set the chile relleno plate in front of Carter, it slid halfway off the table and knocked a mound of Mexican rice onto his lap.

"Oops," the waitress said before walking off.

"Oops? That's it?" Carter's voice was strained. "Not even an *I'm sorry*?" He pointed to the plate in front of him. "And I didn't even order this."

"That's mine." Sienna slid the plate over. "It's okay if some of the rice is gone."

"It's not okay when it's all over my lap," Carter said. "I can't believe my girlfriend is out with another guy right now."

"And you're out with another girl." Sienna gave him a small smile.

"It's not as if I chose this."

"Thanks a lot," she said.

"I didn't mean it like that. It's just that Tracie and I have been dating for so long. We had all these plans." Carter shook his head. "I'm kind of in shock."

She knew that. It was selfish of her to take him all over San Diego tonight just so she could try to make Mark jealous. Poor Carter was in no condition to go anywhere but his own house. "Do you want to head home now?" she asked.

"Do you mind?"

Sienna sighed. "No. No, I don't mind." Tonight she'd not only been rejected by Mark, but by Carter too. Not that she was interested in anyone but Mark tonight. Still, it hurt.

"I can't believe Tracie walked away from me, holding Aaron's hand," Carter said. "In front of everyone."

"I bet she'll be really embarrassed tomorrow. Getting drunk. Acting like that." Sienna put her elbows on the table and her chin atop her hands. "And I can't believe Mark just went off with Lily like that," she said. "We've been dating for almost a year, but he dropped me like it was nothing."

"I know." Carter rubbed his forehead as if he had a headache. "It's not just inconsiderate. It's stupid. Mark should be grateful that a terrific, beautiful girl like you ever went out with him in the first place."

"Thanks." Carter was such a sweetie. She had always liked the way he treated her best friend. But tonight she saw him as something more than just Tracie's boyfriend. Hanging out with him one on one, she realized he was a pretty cool guy. "You know," she told Carter. "Of all the people to spend time with right after my boyfriend dumped me, I'm glad I ended up with you."

He smiled. "You're not so bad yourself, Sienna." They got doggie bags for the food that neither of them had any appetite for, returned to Sienna's car, and headed toward Carter's house. They hardly spoke, but Sienna felt comforted by his presence.

"You okay?" Carter asked as she parked at his house.

She nodded. "I guess I'll drive home and try to get some sleep."

"I'm sorry I couldn't cheer you up," Carter said. "I'm not exactly at the top of my game tonight either. But listen. If you can't sleep and need to talk to someone, you can always call me. I'll probably be up, staring at pictures of Tracie or hitting my head against a wall or doing something equally dopey."

A sweetie even when he's upset, she thought.

"I hope I can get to sleep," Carter said. "At least I'll see Tracie tomorrow, though she'll probably have a major hangover. She asked me a few days ago to keep her company at the band rehearsal tomorrow. I'd like to go out with her tomorrow night too. I mean, if Tracie hasn't already made plans with Aaron. She better not have."

Sienna shook her head. "This whole swapping-guys game really screwed us. No offense."

"It sure did. No offense," Carter said. "I hope both Tracie and Mark realize what huge mistakes they made tonight."

He was such a genuinely nice guy. Too bad she wasn't attracted to him. Though she wouldn't be attracted to Heath Ledger right now if he were here. She couldn't stop thinking about Mark.

"Take care of yourself," Carter said before getting out of the car, heading up his driveway, and letting himself in.

Sienna drove away, sorry to be alone. As she approached her house, Sienna searched for Mark's Camry, hoping he'd realized how foolish he'd been and had driven over to plead for forgiveness. She suspected that was a crazy thought. But she couldn't help it.

No. No Camry. No other cars at all. She blinked back tears again, parked her car, and went inside.

Her parents were already asleep, fortunately. The last thing she wanted was to have to lie to them about what she had done tonight while trying to hide her anguish.

She headed to her bedroom, closed the door, plopped her purse on her desk, and took off her shoes. Then she sat on her bed with her legs crossed. She stared blankly ahead with dead eyes and hugged herself tightly, her fingernails digging into her arms. She wondered what Mark was doing right now. Was he still with Lily? Maybe he'd taken her home hours ago. He was usually so sensible and caring. But tonight he'd acted like an idiot. She hoped he'd realize that soon. Maybe he would call her or come by.

She should call Mark and yell at him. Or should she beg him to come over? She walked to her desk, took her cell phone out of her purse, and returned to her position on the bed, this time with the phone on her lap. She sat like that for a very long time, with no idea what to do.

nine

Mark and Lily were the only two people left on the beach, and Mark felt tongue-tied and clumsy, almost like he had felt while they were waiting to audition earlier today. Being alone with Lily had been a fantasy of his, but now that it had come to pass he didn't know exactly what to do.

"You want to go somewhere?" she asked him.

"How about we take a walk?" Last week he'd dreamed of them on the beach together, hand in hand.

She shrugged. "Okay. I'm easy."

Easy in what way? Mark couldn't help wondering. Then he thought about Sienna and felt guilty. *But she had agreed to trade boyfriends tonight. Maybe she and Carter are hitting it off,* he told himself. But he didn't really believe that.

"You okay?" she asked.

Oh, man. He was blowing it with Lily. He hadn't agreed to

hook up with her just to mope around all night. "I'm great," he said. "Happy to be with you now, and so psyched we aced the audition."

"I'm really happy too," she said.

He didn't know whether Lily meant she was happy about the Waves audition or happy about being with him. He decided it would be too conceited to assume the latter. "I'm going to record a demo of Amber Road and try to get some good managers to listen to it," he said. "And I want to pass out a bunch of flyers advertising our performance at Waves."

"Cool."

"Also, we need to rehearse like crazy. I'll try to write some great new songs, songs that'll show off your amazing voice, Lily."

Lily took Mark's hand. He had to tell himself to breathe. Her hand felt so right in his, so soft but so strong too.

She squeezed it. "Mark, let's not get carried away with rehearsals and stuff. Being in Amber Road is supposed to be a fun thing, not like a serious job."

"It's more fun if you take it seriously," Mark said.

"I don't take anything seriously."

Not even me? Mark wanted to ask. *Of course not. They weren't serious,* he told himself. Lily said this would be just for fun. But what if he wanted something besides fun? He hadn't meant to risk his relationship with Sienna just for one night of fun with Lily. He wasn't that type of guy, anyway. Aaron and George might like to fool around with a bunch of different girls, but Mark wanted something deeper. So why was he here with Lily, a girl who had just told him she didn't take anything seriously? He shrugged. Because he just couldn't help himself around her?

"I'm not into Amber Road as much as you are," Lily continued. "I like being in the group, but I also want time to hang with friends and do other things."

"But I think you could go really far as a singer if you just worked on it more."

"I'd rather spend my time alone with you, looking at the gorgeous sky, than rehearsing with the entire band."

When she put it that way, he completely saw her point. It emboldened him. "I have a blanket in my trunk," he said. "We can spread it over the sand and sit down and watch the sky and the ocean."

She squeezed his hand. "That sounds awesome." Mark hurried to his car and got the blanket.

They laid it about halfway between the car and the water and sat next to each other. Mark couldn't help remembering the last time he'd been on the blanket. He and Sienna had gotten horny and used it at an empty golf course just a few nights ago. He wondered again if he had made a mistake to agree to swap girls. Maybe he should drive to Sienna's house and apologize.

But even while he had made love to Sienna, he'd felt as if his life was missing something. Now he realized it wasn't *something* he'd been missing, it was *someone*. Lily. He put his arm around her shoulder, felt her soft, wavy hair.

"Let's go for a swim," Lily said.

"But I don't have a bathing suit."

She giggled. "So?"

"So let's go." Man, it felt good to say that. He couldn't remember when he'd ever done anything this crazy. He didn't want to remember. Tonight, he'd just focus on having a good time with Lily.

They took off their clothes in the dusk and raced into the

cold ocean, screaming and laughing. He could see her silhouette in the water, and it was even sexier than he'd imagined. And he *had* imagined it. Her body was long and thin, but her chest and hips had nice rounded curves. Better than nice, actually. Beautiful.

Mark and Lily were shivering when they returned to the shore, so they wrapped themselves in the blanket and hugged each other close. They sat on the shore with their chests pressed together and their arms around each other for a very long time. "Thank you," Mark said.

"For what?"

"For suggesting the boyfriend swap. This is turning out to be one of the best nights of my life."

"And I'm glad you suggested staying at the beach together. Look how beautiful it is." Lily pointed upward. "I love when the sky turns red and gold while the sun fades away."

He drew her closer to him. "Man, Lily. That's pretty. You're a poet."

She shook her head. "You think I'm being corny, don't you?"

"I think those words are almost as beautiful as you are. I might even use them in a song, if that's okay."

She smiled softly and sang the lyric she had just spoken.

"You're amazing," he said. "Sing something else."

She shook her head. "Hey, you didn't agree to the swap just to get, like, more rehearsal time out of me, did you?"

He laughed. "It's just that your voice is so awesome. Wait. I just thought of something. How's this for a lyric? 'If it's right, right now, why should I slow down? Don't let me touch the ground tonight.'"

She sang it and Mark shivered with excitement. "I'm going to write some more lyrics, and call this song 'Beautiful Girl,'" he said. His hand played with her thick hair. *It's like hot lava down a mountain,* he thought. *Man, she's so incredible.* Mark had no more doubts about the trade.

"I write songs sometimes," she said. "I never show them to anyone. I sing what I write, but only in private."

"We should write something together," Mark suggested.

"Oh, I'm no good," Lily objected.

"What you said about the sky was fantastic. I bet you could be a great writer if you applied yourself."

"I used to want to be a writer. Not a songwriter. A book writer. An author. When I was a kid I read all the time. Lonely childhood, except for my brother and my books." She laughed.

Mark felt his heart surge. He knew a lonely childhood couldn't have been funny to her.

"I like to read too," he said. As they talked, they realized they shared some favorite authors, and they had the same taste in music. They both loved Red Chimp and Gutwrench, local groups that were not widely known. They each confessed to stage fright before performing, which disappeared once they started singing. Mark couldn't believe his luck. Not only did he and Lily connect fantastically physically, but they connected just as much or more as friends.

Sienna was a lot of fun, but she had never suggested they go skinny-dipping like Lily had. She never made his heart beat so fast. She failed to make every part of his body throb like Lily did. Mark kissed Lily's hair and took in a deep whiff of her tart scent.

Lily put her hands on his cheeks, pushed her mouth against his, and kissed him. Her fast, rough tongue slid deep inside his mouth.

He closed his eyes, leaned into her, and returned her kiss. It was even better than Mark had imagined.

Until he pictured Sienna, her sad eyes tonight that seemed to have been fighting off tears. *How could I do this to her?* he asked himself. *Sienna is a nice girl, and I have a lot in common with her also.* She liked Red Chimp and Gutwrench too. In fact, Sienna had introduced those bands to Mark. And just glancing at her before a performance always soothed Mark's stage fright. At least it used to.

Kissing Lily suddenly left a bad taste in Mark's mouth. He pulled back and said, "Everything's happening too fast. I think we should leave."

ten

Mark paced his soundproofed garage. The door was open as he waited for the other members of Amber Road to arrive. Last night with Lily had been awesome and he hadn't wanted it to end. But he had no idea how long the boyfriend/ girlfriend trade was supposed to last. Soon, Lily and Sienna would be here. He didn't know what either of them expected of him, or what he expected from them. Were he and Lily a couple now? Or was last night just a onetime thing? He had no clue. He did know that he wasn't ready to return to Sienna. He wasn't sure if he'd ever be ready to return to Sienna.

Lily was the first to arrive, wearing a long, low-cut dress so tight it looked like it was difficult to walk in. For a few moments, Mark could not breathe. Shortly after his body recovered from the sight of her, she put her arms around him and kissed him long and deep. Again, he lost his breath. And now he could barely stand.

He closed his eyes and returned her kiss, concentrating only on how good her mouth felt against his.

He heard footsteps. It was idiotic to kiss Lily in his garage with the door wide open and Sienna and the rest of the band expected any moment. He pulled away from Lily and opened his eyes.

George stood frozen on the driveway with his eyebrows raised. Holding his hand was a girl with a cropped haircut and thick black glasses.

At least it wasn't Sienna standing there. "Lily, you're an awesome girl," Mark murmured. "But we shouldn't be kissing here. What if Sienna sees us like this?"

"You sure weren't worried last night," she said.

"Sienna had already left the beach last night," he reminded Lily. When he agreed to the swap, he had worried about his girlfriend, but he hadn't thought about how it would affect Amber Road. If Sienna was mad at Lily and him, he didn't know how the band would get through rehearsal together, let alone a performance at Waves.

George finally walked into the garage with his date. He said, "What in the . . ."

"Hi, guys." Tracie and Aaron walked up the driveway toward them. They held hands and smiled. Mark supposed last night had been good to them, too.

"What in the . . ." George's jaw dropped.

"I guess you had a lucky night, too," Lily said.

"Totally," Tracie said.

"What in the . . ." George asked again.

"Carter's coming." Mark pointed to Carter's Prius moving slowly down the street, then stared hard at Tracie and Aaron's hands until they dropped them to their sides.

"I think I missed something really wild last night," George said. "You guys have an orgy or what? Why didn't you beg me to stay?"

The girl next to him clucked at him and said, "Don't be crass."

"It wasn't like that," Mark tried to explain. "A few minutes after you left, we did this boyfriend swap game."

"Dude, I would have been all over that like *People* magazine on a dead celebrity. Midori and I broke up last night. I think we did, anyway. She doesn't speak English. She kept saying *sayonara.* Anyway, I wish I hadn't left the beach early. I would have been totally available for all kinds of games."

The girl next to him let go of his hand, slapped him, and walked away.

"Mary Sue?" George called after her while rubbing his cheek.

She turned around and wagged her finger at him. "Shame on you."

"Do you want me to at least drive you home?" George asked.

"On that deathmobile you call a motorcycle? I'll call my daddy and get him to pick me up. You'd better hope he doesn't bring his shotgun."

George sighed. "Back to the old drawing board."

"That girl didn't last long," Mark said, patting his friend on the shoulder. "Maybe I should lock up the garage after everyone gets here."

Sienna walked into the garage smiling. *If she knew what I was up to last night,* Mark thought, *she wouldn't be so eager to come here.*

"It's good to see you," Sienna told him as he closed the garage door behind her.

Mark smiled at her, but he felt like the phoniest person outside Hollywood.

"Luckily, I haven't run off with Carter, and you and Lily didn't elope or anything." Sienna reached her arms around him and kissed him. "Mark, I'm so glad that dumb swap thing is over."

"Is it over?" Lily asked calmly.

Mark shrugged. He sure hoped not. But as much as he loved being with Lily last night, the most powerful emotion he felt now was dread. He hated the thought of having to break up with Sienna and upset her.

"What happened last night?" Sienna asked, her voice cracking. Obviously, she already was upset.

"I was with Sienna, and I can promise you we just hung out as friends," Carter said. He put his arm around Tracie. Mark thought he saw her stiffen.

"Do you want to hear about what happened between Tracie and me?" Aaron asked.

"No," Mark said. "Let's do what we're here for and practice our songs. We have to play well at Waves next week."

"Let's start with 'Love Me Like No Other,'" Lily said.

Mark wondered if Lily had suggested that song just to show up Sienna. After all, it was not only a love song, but a duet that Mark had originally written for Sienna. She and Mark used to sing it together before Lily took over as lead singer. But he couldn't object to the song without opening up a can of worms. So he said, "Okay, guys, we'll play 'Love Me Like No Other.' Let's go."

The band members got in their positions and Aaron and Carter sat down—far apart from each other—to listen. Lily made the song more beautiful than it had ever sounded. For the first time, Lily had emotion almost matching her perfect pitch and incredible range. And Mark sang with more passion than ever before. Together they had chemistry to spare.

Unfortunately, Sienna kept messing up on the guitar, coming in early several times and hitting the wrong notes too. Plus, her background vocals were so loud they almost drowned out Lily's exquisite voice.

Mark wondered if it was intentional or if she was so upset about last night that she couldn't focus on the music. No, Sienna was too nice a girl to intentionally impede Amber Road. And it wasn't as if he were rubbing his feelings for Lily in Sienna's face.

When the song ended, Aaron said, "I never heard you sing better, Lily."

"Whatever happened last night at least paid off in your performance today," George said. "What exactly did happen during that boyfriend swap game, anyway? If you guys had an orgy without me, I'll never forgive you. Unless you promise to invite me to the next one."

Mark shook his head. "We didn't have any orgies."

"Speak for yourself," Aaron said, and Carter shot him a hateful look.

"We can talk later. We don't want to lose our momentum," Mark said. "Let's switch it up to a song that really rocks. 'School's Out' first, and then we can go right into 'Partytime.'"

Everyone returned to the music. Except Tracie, who missed

her first cue. She was staring at Aaron, specifically at his chest beneath a T-shirt so tight it practically looked shrink-wrapped onto his torso.

"Come on, Tracie, pay attention," Mark complained. He didn't mean to sound so sour, but the upcoming Waves gig made him nervous.

They tried again and Tracie missed her cue again.

Sienna seemed distracted too. She kept looking at Lily and Mark with pursed lips. Sienna must have realized that things had changed last night. She was usually so focused and driven at rehearsals, but today she played as if her mind were on everything *but* the music.

Mark's soundproofed garage was big enough to accommodate all five members of the band, their equipment, and Aaron and Carter. But even a football stadium couldn't contain the tension and wandering thoughts among the band members today.

Mark decided to shake things up. "Guys, let's try a song we hardly ever rehearse. You all remember 'Stray Cat'?"

"Meow!" Tracie said.

Aaron sidled over to her and stroked her cheek. "I bet I could make you purr."

"Stop it." Tracie grabbed his wrist and took his hand off her face. But she was smiling while she did it. She might as well have pressed his hand onto her cheek and said, *Keep going.* Mark rolled his eyes.

"Whatever love potion you two drank, I want some of it," George said.

"I think it's a *lust* potion, not a love potion," Sienna said dryly.

"That's it. I've had it." Carter stood up. "Tracie, I have better things to do than watch you flirt with Aaron. Once you start acting like you have a boyfriend, you know where I live." He stormed out of the garage.

"I should go after him," Tracie said without moving.

Sienna nodded. "You should. I can imagine how betrayed he feels right now." She looked at Mark and Lily as she spoke. "What ever happened to loyalty to the person you're dating?"

"Carter will get over it. He's a big boy." Aaron rose from his seat, stood behind Tracie, and put his hands around her little waist. She leaned into him. She apparently wasn't going after Carter, or anywhere else.

"Let's get on with rehearsal," Mark said. "One, two, three, go." He sang, "You're slinky like a stray."

Lily joined in. "If I don't stray I'll move away. 'Cause I like to run out at night."

She had a unique voice, soft and feminine but at the same time sultry and strong. *Just like her personality,* Mark thought.

He sang, "Come into my room tonight, my cat."

She sang, "I'll behave in the day, but at night I like to straaaay."

Man, she was sexy. He wondered what it would be like to make love to her. He made himself focus on the song.

But Tracie and Sienna obviously were focused on other things. Tracie whispered something to Aaron, completely missing her cue. Meanwhile, Sienna was strumming way too hard on bass. Mark thought he and George and Lily sounded great, but Amber Road's success depended on every one of its members performing their best.

At the end of the song, Mark put his hand up. "Guys,

please, we have to try a lot harder. Our big shot is coming up at Waves."

"Who's coming to hear you?" Aaron interrupted. "Anyone I know?"

Mark's teeth clenched. Aaron wasn't in the band and shouldn't even be here. Not only had he been distracting Tracie since they arrived together hand in hand, but now he was interrupting Mark's attempt to give the band a much-needed pep talk.

"Whitney Lowell said she'd come," Lily said. "And you know how popular Whitney is at our school. Like a queen bee. If she decides to hear a band, all her hangers-on at school will want to also."

"Guys, listen to me, please." Mark cleared his throat.

"Whitney Lowell has amazing style," Aaron said. "She always looks hot."

"Her wardrobe is hot, I'll give her that. She must spend a fortune on clothes." Tracie crossed her arms. "But take away all her high-fashion outfits and thick makeup, and I think she'd be kind of plain-looking."

"Uh-oh. Trouble in boyfriend swap paradise already?" George asked.

Mark couldn't help hoping. Aaron seemed like a total player. Maybe Tracie was realizing this now.

"Of course, Whitney's not as hot as Tracie." Aaron obviously was trying to cover for himself. "No one's as hot as my gorgeous Tracie."

Lily is, Mark said to himself. He thought Lily was the sexiest girl alive. But he wasn't about to announce this, not in front of Sienna. He stared at Lily, at her bright eyes and sweet lips and willowy figure. It wasn't just her great looks and incredible singing that made her special. She was so much fun too. He remembered skinny-dipping last night and smiled. The most exciting thing he'd done with Sienna lately had been to go to the movies.

Mark shook his head. He'd been thinking about Lily instead of the band, getting just as distracted as Tracie and Sienna were today. How could he make them concentrate on Amber Road if he himself wasn't paying attention? He forced his gaze away from Lily and his thoughts away from her naked body in the dark ocean last night. "Let's rehearse 'Stray Cat' again," he announced. "Please, everyone, try your best."

They started the song and Lily sounded better than ever.

For God's sake. Tracie missed her cue again. And Sienna's rhythm was completely off.

Aaron laughed. "My deaf grandmother could play a better bass guitar than you today, Sienna."

"I've had it with you, Aaron! Why the hell are you here, anyway?" Sienna shouted. "You aren't in our damn band." She grabbed one of George's drumsticks and threw it at Aaron.

He ducked, and it landed by his foot.

The rest of the band froze. Mark knew Sienna should be stopped, and he was supposed to be in charge of Amber Road; but he also felt as if he deserved to suffer Sienna's wrath.

Aaron yelled back at her. "Listen, you bi—"

"Hey, stop this, both of you," Mark interrupted. Now things had gotten completely out of hand. "Aaron, why don't you go home? I think we should make rehearsals a band-members-only thing from now on."

"He's my brother." Lily crossed her arms.

Tracie grabbed Aaron's hand. "He should be able to stay. Like it or not."

"Well, I don't like it. You have awful taste in guys," Sienna said.

"You sure seem to like Carter a lot," Tracie replied. "You had your chance with him at the beach last night."

"Some people are loyal to their boyfriends. I guess you can't understand that. Mark and Lily don't get it either." Sienna glared at them. "It makes me sick."

What have I done? Mark asked himself. He had never heard Sienna sound so angry. It wasn't just anger, he knew. He had hurt her too.

"Do you ever shut up, Sienna?" Aaron said.

"It makes *me* sick that I'm giving up part of my Saturday to practice really hard for the sake of this band, and you keep screwing up your part," Lily said. "You're bringing us down, Sienna."

She had a point, Mark thought, but did she have to be so harsh? Especially since she was the one who had organized last night's trade, which had upset everything.

"As if I feel any sympathy for someone who's trying to steal my boyfriend from me," Sienna responded.

"Don't drag my sister into your stupid catfight," Aaron said.

"Did someone mention a catfight? Should I get my camera?" George joked.

Nobody laughed.

"Your sister has no morals," Sienna said.

"Shut up! Don't you dare talk about Lily like that." Aaron picked up the drumstick, rushed to George's drum, and banged on it. He hit it so hard he dented the snare.

Mark could hardly breathe. Up until last night, they had all gotten along. Now they were screaming at each other, throwing things, damaging instruments. Less than twenty-four hours ago they had been celebrating their success. Now it seemed as if they were on the road to ruin.

"Look what you've done!" Sienna shouted at Aaron. "You dented George's drum."

Aaron shrugged. "No big deal. I didn't do it on purpose."

"Bull," Sienna said.

"You're the one who hurled the drumstick at me," Aaron said.

"That's because you—"

"Shut it already. I'm sorry, okay?" He pulled a money clip from his front pocket and handed George a hundred-dollar bill. "That should cover it."

"I'm out of here," Sienna said.

"Sienna," Mark said.

"Don't even talk to me." She gathered up her guitar and music sheets and purse. "Do you know how agonizing this is for me? Having Aaron here mouthing off, while you're making puppy-dog eyes at Lily? I don't need to put up with all the crap going on here." She started carrying her equipment out of the garage.

"Please, Sienna." Tracie took a step toward her friend.

"Just let her go," Aaron said.

"We can work this out," Mark said, not sure that they really could.

Sienna walked out of the garage.

Tracie and Mark followed her, but she yelled at them to go away.

Mark returned to his garage and said, "I guess rehearsal's

over." He stood at the entrance with his arms crossed, shaking his head. Was there any chance that Sienna could perform with them at Waves on Thursday? Even if she did, would Amber Road be able to deliver a solid set, free of flaws and personal drama? Mark had grave doubts on both counts. If Amber had heard the band today—messing up on their instruments, yelling at each other, throwing things, stalking out of the rehearsal—she probably would have wished they'd never used her name.

eleven

Tracie sat on her bed Sunday morning and finished the solo on "School's Out." She thought it sounded decent—better than her halfhearted attempts at rehearsal—but that didn't stop her from worrying. Amber Road had bombed yesterday, and their Waves performance was only four days away.

She should practice some more, or maybe work on the paper due in AP English tomorrow. But she stayed on the bed doing nothing but gripping her guitar.

She wished she had someone to talk to right now. Carter was at the debate tournament. Besides, they hadn't spoken since yesterday, after he'd seen Aaron flirting with her and left the rehearsal. Sienna would be at church still. Once services ended, she'd probably go to Mark's house as she usually did on Sundays.

Thank God she and Sienna had talked things out last night.

She didn't know who was more stressed: Sienna, totally hurt over Mark and Lily; or herself, feeling like a horrible person for fooling around on Carter, but at the same time excited about Aaron.

She had always imagined herself as a faithful and loyal girl-friend. But by the end of their date, when she and Aaron had their hands and mouths all over each other, her nice image of herself had been completely shattered. At least Sienna had reassured her that her date with Carter had been purely platonic.

Tracie strummed the guitar a few times, then put it down. She couldn't focus on her music now.

She walked to her desk and e-mailed Sienna.

Hey. Our girls' nite out was fun last nite. Who needs guys, anyway? We do! Still torn up about Aaron. I know u think he's bad, but he was sooo sweet Friday nite. Hope yr feeling better about M and L. I bet they won't even last past this weekend. M probably misses u like crazy.
U think we should all try to rehearse again today? Me & u could still go to the mall like we talked about, & I could write the stupid Dickens paper late tonite if I have to.
Let me know.
T

After she sent the e-mail to Sienna, she thought about e-mailing everyone in Amber Road. She should apologize for her poor playing yesterday and suggest that they all rehearse again today. She sure didn't want Amber Road to blow their one opportunity at Waves Thursday night.

There was a knock on her bedroom door. "A young man is at the front door for you," her mother called out.

A young man? Tracie was sure it wasn't Carter. He was at the debate finals in L.A. today. Besides, her mother knew him so well she wouldn't have called him a "young man."

Was it Mark? Maybe he was arranging another rehearsal after yesterday's disaster. Or what if Aaron was here? She hadn't planned on going out with him again. Their Friday night date at the pool hall was fantastic, maybe too fantastic. She had a boyfriend.

Carter was a very nice guy. He didn't deserve a girlfriend who fooled around on him. Shooting pool with Aaron was one thing; making out with him afterward was different. It was just plain wrong. She was committed to Carter, or at least supposed to be. In about six months she and Carter would move cross-country to attend college together. Eventually, they'd probably marry and start a family together. At least that's what everyone always seemed to assume. Seeing Aaron could ruin her lifetime plans. Were they *her* plans, though? Or had she just gone along with Carter and everyone else?

That might not even be Aaron at the door. He wasn't the only "young man" she knew. But if it was him, Carter didn't have to find out because he was out of town today. What he didn't know wouldn't hurt him. And maybe if Tracie were to date other guys, she'd learn to appreciate Carter more. This could be just what their relationship needed.

She was lying to herself. But she couldn't resist the opportunity to go out with Aaron again.

She stood up and rushed to the mirror on her bedroom door. She frowned. She hadn't put on makeup yet and she thought she looked washed out.

"Tracie, are you coming?" her mother called out.

Oh, God. If it was Aaron at the door and he was talking to

her parents right now, they'd probably be shaking their heads as they stared at his tight T-shirt and bulging biceps and expensive ripped jeans, and listened to his stories about his wild times in Europe. They'd probably move her curfew to eight o'clock, or lock her in the house until she turned eighteen. Tracie swiped pink lipstick across her lips and brown mascara on her lashes and rushed to the front door, hoping that the "young man" was Aaron and that he hadn't shocked her mom and dad, who were used to Carter the model citizen.

It was Aaron. The poor guy sat on the living room couch surrounded by her parents, one on each side. Lord help him.

She came closer and saw his outfit. Instead of Aaron's usual getup, today he wore a button-down striped shirt and khakis.

"Hi, Aaron." Tracie tried to seem casual. She really wanted to burst out laughing at his clothes and then sit on his lap and kiss him. But that would probably give her parents simultaneous strokes.

"Tracie," her father said. "I didn't know you were going to the library today."

The library? What? Now Tracie put her hand over her mouth to hold in the threatening hysterical laughter. Had Aaron Bouchet ever even been in a library before?

"Aaron says you two are working on a history project," her mother said.

"Oh, sorry." Tracie couldn't look at her parents. "I guess I forgot to tell you about the project," she managed to say.

"We might be at the library for hours," Aaron said. "I want to do a great job to keep up my four-point-two GPA."

He was good! Tracie would be surprised if his GPA were over 3.0. She didn't know how much longer she could keep a straight face. "Is it okay if I go now?" Tracie asked her mother.

"Of course, dear." Her mother smiled. "Though I wish you kids wouldn't spend all your time studying. This is the weekend, after all."

"Maybe we can take a break for lunch, then return to the library afterward and start typing up our research on the computer," Aaron said.

"Aaron works so hard to get what he wants," Tracie said. She noticed his lip curling up, fighting a smile. "Straight A's, I mean. That's what Aaron wants. Well, we'd better get going so we can snag good seats at the library."

Her father cocked his head. "I didn't know it was open this early on a Sunday."

Before Tracie could start seriously panicking about getting caught in a lie, Aaron said, "I called around and found one that opens at nine."

Wow, the guy was smooth.

"Smart thinking. You need money for lunch?" Her father handed her a twenty.

She almost didn't want to take it from him. Almost. Tracie knew they'd better leave before they told too many more lies. She excused herself to get her backpack from her bedroom. Once there, she stuffed it with old magazines about the same size as the history textbook in her school locker. She also dabbed perfume onto her neck and shoulders and put rouge on her cheeks.

She was able to keep a straight face all the way out of her house. But once she closed the front door, she started giggling. Her giggles turned into guffaws when she got in Aaron's Porsche, and she could hardly hold herself up after Aaron removed his button-down shirt to reveal a tight black T-shirt.

As he pulled away, he put his hand on the inside of her

thigh. Tracie knew she wouldn't be seeing the interior of a library any time today. "You're good," she said.

He moved his hand almost to her crotch. "I'd like to show you how good I am."

"I bet you're wonderful. But today's way too soon to show me." She moved his hand lower on her leg. "Where are we really going?"

"Don't worry, babe. I have it all planned." As he drove, it started to rain. He moved his hand on her leg in rhythm with the slow swishing of the windshield wipers.

She reached over and put her hand on his leg too. God, his thigh was so muscular. She bet he really was wonderful in bed. But she had held on to her virginity for so many years with Carter, she wasn't about to lose it on her second date with Aaron. That's what she kept reminding herself, anyway, as her body ached with yearning.

Her cell phone rang. She fished it out of her purse and checked to see who was calling. Sienna. She sighed and picked up. Her left hand remained on Aaron's hard leg, while he stroked her thigh. "What's up?" she said into the phone.

"Hey, girl," Sienna said. "I just got out of church. I'm heading to Mark's house in a few minutes. You think I should go to Mark's today, right?" Her voice quivered. "It's been pretty much our routine on Sundays."

"If he's expecting you to show up, then, yeah." Tracie wasn't sure that he was. Mark and Lily had been making eyes at each other all during yesterday's rehearsal.

Aaron clamped his hand hard around the inside of her thigh. She looked at him, at his dark, dramatic eyes and rugged face. How could she give Sienna advice when she could hardly think about anything except how much she liked Aaron's hand on her leg? "Sorry, Sienna, but I have to get off the phone," Tracie said.

"Oh, okay. What time are we meeting at the mall today? Four o'clock too late?"

"The mall?" Tracie said loudly.

Aaron pouted and whispered in her ear, "I've got the whole day planned."

So she said, "Gee, I can't make it today."

Now Aaron was smiling at her and mouthing, "Thanks."

"And I really need to get off the phone, Sienna."

"But, Tracie—"

"Let's talk tonight for sure. I hope everything goes okay for you today," she said before clicking off her cell phone.

"Could you leave it off?" Aaron asked. "Please?"

"Okay, I will." She turned off her phone and threw it in her purse. She'd have to call Sienna later and apologize. She hoped her friend would understand.

"I guarantee you I'll show you a better time than you'd have talking on the phone or hanging around the mall." He moved his hand far up the inside of her thigh again, and she pushed it down again.

He grinned. "Gorgeous and feisty. I like that in a girl."

She smiled back at him. If he kept calling her *gorgeous*, he'd wear down her feistiness.

He headed southwest, getting off the freeway near Point Loma and taking the windy road with its gorgeous ocean views. He parked at the marina and said, "Let's take a walk."

"But I didn't bring my umbrella," Tracie said.

Aaron shrugged. "Neither did I. It's a warm rain, and I bet you look just as gorgeous when you're wet."

She got out of the Porsche and Aaron put his arm around

her. He was right, it was a warm rain. The weather didn't bother her. She didn't think anything could bother her while Aaron had his strong arm across her back.

They strode past the little fish market and tackle shop and boat-chartering business to the marina, which was deserted. Most people in Southern California didn't venture out when it rained. They walked up the boardwalk to the docks, still arm in arm. Aaron let go of her and stepped onto a large yacht called *Dena Kate*. He reached over and held out his hand for her to grasp.

She stayed on the dock. "Your family owns this boat?" she asked.

"Not exactly," Aaron said. "But don't worry. I come here all the time. It's practically mine."

Tracie kept her hands to her sides. She knew that *practically mine* wasn't the same thing as *mine*. This had to be illegal. Trespassing. Maybe breaking and entering. Probably other violations too.

He looked so handsome standing on the boat, his thick hair midnight-black from the rain, his wet shirt pressed tight against his skin, revealing in fine detail his magnificent chest, his pecs bulging as he extended his arm to her.

She took a deep breath, then put her hand into his and said, "Okay."

As soon as he helped her onto the boat, he said, "Let's get out of the rain." He lead her to a narrow, steep staircase as if he knew exactly where he was going. She followed him down.

The cabin had a maroon leather love seat, a small wooden table with two chairs, a bar and sink and mini-fridge, and even a washer and dryer. Tracie stood at the porthole watching the rain agitate the sea.

When she looked back at Aaron a minute or so later, his T-shirt was on the floor by his feet and he was removing his loafers and socks. Tracie crossed her arms in front of her. "What are you doing?"

"Don't worry, babe. I'll leave my boxers on. I'm just going to put my wet clothes in the dryer. You want me to dry your clothes too?"

"I'm a virgin, and I plan to stay that way for a while," Tracie said as firmly as she could.

"Of course," Aaron said as if he had never intended otherwise.

So she stripped down to her bra and underwear. They put their clothes in the dryer, opened a bottle of red wine Aaron found in a cupboard, and sat together on the love seat arm in arm, the pounding of the rain and the tumbling of the dryer in the background. *Another first,* she thought as she sipped the wine. She liked this better than beer. It was sweet and flowed smoothly down her throat and made her feel tingly. As she snuggled next to Aaron, with his rough body against her pale, soft skin, she couldn't help thinking, *This sure beats studying in my room and hanging with Sienna,* which was what she had planned for today.

She had almost finished her second glass of wine when she asked Aaron, "You're not going to try anything?"

"Not if you don't want me to," he said. "Though would you be offended if I said you have a gorgeous body to match your gorgeous face?"

She smiled. "You're not so bad yourself, you know." She stared at him, at his tan, muscular chest, his tight stomach, and his damp boxers, which showed him to great advantage. *Huge advantage,* Tracie said to herself.

"We can just sit here and talk and put our clothes back on as soon as they're dry," he said.

But next to him, almost naked, she was nearly dying. She wanted to kiss him so bad. "How about I just sit on your lap?" she asked.

He smirked at her. "Only if you really want to."

"I want to. I really want to." She straddled his lap again, as she'd done in his car. But this time they were both still a little wet and half naked. She kissed him, and he unclasped her bra and threw it onto the floor, and she suspected that she would not be keeping her virginity much longer.

twelve

Sienna slowly walked up Mark's driveway. Her parents had dropped her off here after church, as was their Sunday morning custom. She and Mark would attempt to write songs, talk about ways to improve and promote Amber Road, eat lunch, and usually make out in Mark's bedroom.

But there was no *usually* anymore. Something had happened between Mark and Lily the night of the boyfriend swap. That they had connected somehow, in a big way, had been obvious at yesterday's practice.

Sienna had spent more than two hours at the hairdresser's yesterday, getting her hair done in cornrows and tiny braids with glassy beads at the end of them. Mark loved when she wore her hair like that. She'd been hoping to see him last night, but he hadn't answered his cell phone. Sienna had no clue what

Mark had been up to and who he'd been with. For all Sienna knew, Mark and Lily had spent last night together too.

"What's wrong?" her mom called out as Sienna ambled up the driveway.

Sienna turned around. The car window was open and her mom's head was hanging halfway out.

"Nothing's wrong!" Sienna shouted. She rushed to the front door, planted on a bright smile, and knocked.

It took a while for him to answer. When he finally opened the door for her, he wore a somber expression. "Hey."

Didn't he notice her special hairstyle? Sienna forced her smile to remain. "Hi! You feel like working on songs?"

He shrugged. "Sure."

She turned around with her fake smile still on, though it hurt her cheeks, and waved to her parents. She watched their car pull away before following Mark into his garage.

"I was thinking we should make some flyers promoting our performance at Waves," she said. She hoped Mark would think about how much she did for Amber Road—a lot more than Lily had ever done.

"We printed up some flyers yesterday, after you left."

"Oh. Good." We? Who was the *we* that made the flyers? Mark and Lily? When she walked out of rehearsal yesterday, she'd just given Lily another opportunity to get Mark alone.

"Can you help hang the flyers at school this week?" he asked.

She forced another smile. "Sure." She cleared her throat. "Let's write some songs."

"We were working on 'Rays of Sun' last week. Should we continue with that?" Mark's voice sounded so formal.

"Okay. How's everything going with you?" she asked.

He nodded. "Fine. You?"

Her smile fled. "Good," she said in a restrained tone to match his. What was going on with him? Had Lily already made him forget how great they were together?

They read over the first two stanzas they'd written before. Then they were quiet for an uncomfortable amount of time—uncomfortable at least for Sienna. She broke the silence by suggesting a few more lines. Each time, Mark said, "That sounds good," and she wrote them down. He didn't share any ideas of his own. He barely looked at her. He'd occasionally glance in her direction, but his eyes wouldn't meet hers.

Sienna decided to wait for him to talk. But he volunteered nothing. So they both stayed silent a long time. Sienna wondered if he was thinking about Lily, how beautiful she was, and confident and sophisticated and wild. He just stared at the song notes they'd written, poker-faced. Finally, Sienna broke down. "Did you go out with Lily last night?" she asked.

He didn't respond.

"Mark, did you?"

He nodded without looking at her.

She felt her hand tighten on the pen. "What did you guys do?"

"Saw a movie."

No. Not the one they were planning to see before Mark decided to go to the beach and do that terrible boyfriend swap instead. He wouldn't have watched that movie with Lily, would he? Sienna had to know. "The horror movie we talked about before?"

He nodded.

"Was it good?" Her voice sounded choked. She felt as if she were choking. She was torturing herself.

"It was okay," he said.

She wondered if he had even watched the screen. Maybe he was making out with Lily the whole time. Her fist clenched. She felt like thrusting it into a wall. Or better yet, into Mark and Lily.

She put her hand behind her back. She wouldn't let them get to her. She was strong. She told herself that, anyway. Yes, strong. She took a deep breath and said, "You know, Carter and I went out on Friday night."

His poker face didn't change.

She had to stay strong. "But we did something more exciting than see a movie. Actually, Carter and I did a lot of things that night. We drove around town and went to a bar and then to this Mexican restaurant. It was awesome." She studied Mark's face for signs of jealousy—furrowed eyebrows, narrowed eyes, red cheeks, anything.

There was none of that. He said, calmly and distantly, "Glad to hear it."

How could he be glad? Unless he couldn't wait to shove her onto someone else so he could be with Lily guilt-free. Was that it? She wanted him to tell her everything. Whose idea was it to get together last night, Mark's or Lily's? Did they hold hands? Did Mark put his arm around Lily as soon as they sat down in the theater and rest it on her shoulder, as he did with her? Did they kiss? How in the world could Mark betray her like that? What had she done wrong? Was there any hope for them now?

She wanted to ask him everything, but she didn't know if she could bear hearing his answers. She felt tears welling. She was not strong, no matter how much she tried to persuade herself that she was. She would cry if they talked about Lily.

She would cry even if they didn't. She couldn't let Mark see that. She might have lost her boyfriend; she didn't want to lose her pride too. "I'd better go," she mumbled.

"Okay," he said with the most enthusiasm he'd shown since he'd arrived. "Hey, do you think we could get people to rehearse today? Our Waves gig is only four days away."

Sienna turned away from him, made her hands into fists, shoved them against her eyes to keep the tears inside, and took a deep breath. "I know Tracie can't rehearse. I just talked to her and she's really busy today."

"We should have organized this sooner," Mark said.

"I tried to phone you last night, but you didn't pick up," Sienna complained. She hadn't been calling to arrange a rehearsal, but still.

"We shouldn't try to practice together without Tracie. She's the one who kept making mistakes yesterday. Tracie and . . ." He trailed off.

You, Sienna, she knew he wanted to say. *Tracie and you both really blew it.* She dabbed at the corners of her eyes. "Okay, well, good-bye," she said hesitantly, hoping Mark would ask her to stay.

"Bye," he said without looking up. He remained at his desk and stared at their song notes as she stood, shuffled toward the door, and left the garage.

Sienna managed to hold in her tears until she was outside. As soon as the door closed, they trickled down her face. She walked to the curb and wondered how she'd get home. She could call her parents, ask them to pick her up. But then she'd have to explain why she hadn't stayed long at Mark's, why he wasn't driving her home as he usually did. She swiped at her cheeks. The tears kept falling. Maybe she should walk. She could sort things out, or at least try to. She started up the street, toward her home. But she was in her church clothes and two-inch heels. And her house was miles away. Her shoulders hunched, then shook. She was having trouble breathing. But she kept walking. She couldn't think of anything else to do. She could barely think at all.

About three blocks from Mark's house she saw a turquoise Jag, Lily's car. Lily was looking into the rearview mirror while putting on lipstick. No doubt she was heading straight for Mark's house. Sienna didn't think Lily even noticed her as she passed by.

The trickle of tears turned into a torrent. It got so bad she couldn't see in front of her. She stopped and sat on the sidewalk. It occurred to her that she was probably ruining her dress. She didn't ever want to wear this dress again, anyway.

She took her phone out of her purse and managed to call Tracie. Sienna felt in a tiny way blessed. No matter what else happened, she had Tracie, and Tracie would always be her friend.

I'm coming to get you, she imagined Tracie saying. *I'll be right there, and then we can figure out how you can get Mark back. And I can go to the mall with you later, after all. Don't worry, Sienna, together we'll make things better.*

But Tracie's cell phone rang and rang.

Sienna kept her phone against her ear, put her head down, and sobbed even harder, right there on the sidewalk.

Later, much later, she threw the phone into her purse, stood up, and continued the long walk home.

thirteen

It was Tuesday after school. Tracie got out another flyer publicizing Amber Road's performance at Waves Thursday night. She had been posting them all over school. She rushed toward the bulletin board near her locker. This would have to be the last flyer she'd put up today because she was supposed to meet Aaron at his car in a few minutes.

She couldn't wait to see him again. But at the same time, she felt guilty. Not only had she not officially broken up with Carter, but she'd turned down band practice for today's date with Aaron.

The Waves performance was just two nights away, and Amber Road hadn't practiced since that awful rehearsal on Saturday. Usually, Mark and Sienna organized the rehearsals together. But when Tracie had returned Sienna's call late

Sunday night, Sienna had told her she was so upset with Mark she couldn't even talk to him without choking up.

So Tracie had called him herself and offered to organize a rehearsal for Monday. But Mark, who up until now had seemed to live and breathe for Amber Road, said he had other plans. When Tracie brought up rehearsing with the other band members, he said Lily had plans on Monday also. It didn't take a genius to figure out that Mark and Lily had scheduled a date together.

Tracie had been left temporarily speechless. It was so beyond Mark's character to choose to go out rather than rehearse. For Mark to give Lily priority ahead of the band meant that he must be crazy about her. Tracie felt terrible for Sienna.

"We could rehearse Tuesday after school," Mark had offered. But Tracie had already made plans with Aaron. *If Mark and Lily can go out instead of getting ready for our big night at Waves,* Tracie told herself recklessly, *I can do the same.*

And so here it was, Tuesday, and the band needed to practice but she was going to see Aaron instead. She didn't regret her decision to choose him over rehearsal, and over Carter. *At least I'm helping Amber Road with publicity,* she thought as she searched for a spare tack to hang the flyer.

"Tracie."

She turned around. "Carter." Did she sound as unhappy by his presence as she felt? "What after-school activity do you have today?" God, she sounded snide. She hadn't meant to.

"I was hoping to talk to you, that's all."

She stuck the poster onto the bulletin board, then made herself face Carter. She couldn't look him in the eye, though. She had been avoiding him at school the last two days. She hadn't even called him after he'd stormed out of rehearsal on Saturday. "I really need to go. I'm supposed to meet someone," Tracie said.

"Who? Never mind. I don't think I want to know." He brushed aside some of his thick, blond hair that had fallen across his forehead.

Tracie used to love putting her fingers through his hair. Now she checked her watch. One more minute before she was supposed to meet Aaron. "I'm going to be late," she told Carter. "I'm sure we'll see each other in school tomorrow, though."

"And when we do, you'll probably avoid me again, right?"

She looked away, not wanting to see the hurt in his eyes.

"Tracie, I need to know what's going on with you— with us."

The truth was that she didn't know. As of now, she was crazy about Aaron, enough to make her want to break up with Carter right away. Sunday—drinking and talking and making out on the yacht with Aaron—had been one of the best days of her life. She was still a virgin, barely, but he had made her feel amazing. And it wasn't just a physical thing. Aaron was a lot of fun too. But even though she longed to be with him, she also knew it was foolish to throw away a three-year relationship with Carter for a guy she'd just started dating five days ago.

So she did a wimpy thing. She said, "I'll tell you what's going on soon, but not today because I'm in a hurry." Then she rushed away without looking back, even after Carter called out, "Tracie, please! Talk to me!"

By the time she got to the school parking lot, Aaron was sitting in his red Porsche with the top down, listening to heavy metal music and playing a game on his cell phone.

"Sorry I'm late," she said.

He smiled. "Come on in and give me a kiss, gorgeous girl, and if it's good enough, maybe I'll forgive you."

So she did, and any thoughts about Amber Road and Carter left her mind.

Being with Aaron was even better than she had imagined, and she had imagined it plenty. They drove to Pacific Beach and walked down the boardwalk hand in hand, dodging bicyclists, Rollerbladers, and drunks sitting on the concrete ledge with paper bags covering bottles of booze. Amid all the commotion around them, Tracie felt a sense of companionship and belonging with Aaron. His hand holding hers was so strong, and she felt so right next to him.

He shouted protectively when a skateboarder almost clipped Tracie, smiled at a chattering baby leaning forward in a stroller, stopped to watch a heated volleyball game on the beach. She had walked down the P.B. boardwalk before, but had never enjoyed it so much.

They hung at a party at a beach house rental filled with college kids, and helped themselves to beer from a keg on the patio. Tracie was getting used to the dense, salty flavor of it. She didn't consider beer exactly tasty now, but she could drink it without making a face. It took them a long time to walk back along the boardwalk and the side streets to Aaron's Porsche because they kept stopping to kiss.

Then Aaron drove to the movie theater while Tracie called her parents and said she was doing more research at the library with Aaron. "He's so intense," she told them as his hand roamed her body.

He bought tickets to a slapstick teen comedy without asking her first. She liked a guy who could take charge. She would never have seen something like that with Carter. He used to study the movie reviews fastidiously, reasoning that it was a waste of their time to see anything with poor write-ups. The movie Aaron was taking her to got only one star from the San Diego newspaper critic, according to Carter.

Carter. She didn't want to think about him, not when she was having such a fantastic time with Aaron.

She ended up liking the movie, even though it was inane. She'd probably enjoy any movie with Aaron sitting next to her. They fed each other Raisinets and licked chocolate from each other's fingers. She laughed and groaned and cuddled with him, and fended off his hand a couple of times when it strayed below her waist. She had made out with Aaron in his car Friday night and had gone further with him on the boat on Sunday, but she was still hanging on to her virginity, ever so precariously.

After the movie, they had a very late dinner. Aaron took her to a Middle Eastern restaurant and ordered for both of them. She sat next to him in a booth, tasting foods she'd never heard of before and watching belly dancers shake their hips to strange, sultry music. "This is so much fun." She kissed Aaron on the cheek.

"It's the company that's great." He turned his face and kissed her hard on the mouth.

This was so different from what she usually did with Carter on a school night. If they managed to see each other at all, it was usually to study. Tracie had barely opened a book since she'd started seeing Aaron. But she felt like she deserved a break.

After they kissed a while at their booth, Aaron pointed to the stage. "That's hot." A girl with thick black hair even longer than Lily's moved her hips in rhythm to a slow song that featured the flute and a strange, high-pitched chant.

"I bet she's wearing a wig," Tracie said.

"I was talking about the jewelry on her belly button. What a turn-on," Aaron said.

"Thanks a lot," Tracie said.

"Of course, she's not as hot as you." Aaron hurriedly reassured her. "No one's as sexy as you. You know you're the most gorgeous girl in the world." He put his arm around her and drew her close, but Tracie didn't feel so gorgeous now. She didn't have diamonds in her stomach like the girl on stage did. She was such a goody-goody.

"Tracie, you are totally red-hot." Aaron said, but his gaze was on the belly dancer. She tried to tell herself it was okay that he was staring at the stage. There was a show going on, after all.

Once it ended, Aaron wanted to drive to "look at the view" off Torrey Pines Road.

But Tracie begged off, saying that she was really tired and that tomorrow was a school day. "Could you please just drive me home?"

"Of course, gorgeous," Aaron said, and he drove her to her house, kissed her lightly, and sped off. He didn't walk her to the front door like Carter always had, but Tracie decided that was a silly tradition. She was perfectly capable of walking up the driveway to her own house. Though she did wish Aaron had waited until she got inside safely before he drove off.

It didn't matter. Her parents were home, and they let her in right away. She spent a few minutes chatting with them. They didn't suspect a thing. "The library was noisy, but Aaron and I got a lot done," she lied. "He's really pushing me to go all the way—all the way with our project so we can get an A." She was getting to be quite an actress, or liar, depending on how you phrased it.

"That's great," her mother said.

Her dad ruffled her hair. "But I want you to have fun too. You've already been accepted at Yale. You should let loose a bit during your last year of high school."

"I'll try." She hid a smile.

After her parents went to bed, Tracie sneaked out of the house. She drove to a strip mall downtown, got out of the car, drew in a deep breath, and walked toward Pedro's Tattoos and Piercings. She hoped they pierced navels there.

fourteen

On Wednesday, Sienna sat at the school lunch table across from Tracie, who was practically bouncing on the bench and grinning like a cheerleader at a pep rally. Sienna could cope with her friend's enthusiasm, but she hoped nobody else would join them. The last thing she needed was to watch Tracie and Aaron make out, or Mark and Lily look like they would be making out if Sienna weren't there. The only member of Amber Road who hadn't managed to upset her these days was George, and George didn't go to their school. She gritted her teeth.

"How's it going? You feeling any better?" Tracie asked her.

Sienna shrugged. "A little better, but that's not saying much. How about you?"

"Fantastic, actually. All because of Aaron. He's so much

fun. And cute and sweet and romantic and sexy and oh my God." She giggled.

Sienna knew she should be happy for her best friend, but it was hard to be happy about anything these days. Besides, Aaron might be an exciting guy, but she didn't respect him, trust him, or particularly like him. "Hey, Tracie, you didn't lose your virginity to him, did you?"

"Of course not," she said. "We've been going out less than a week."

Sienna lifted her eyebrows. "So you *are* going out. It wasn't just a game for one night?"

"I guess it started out as a game, but it's moved on from there. Now we're serious."

"And yet you've been going out less than a week," Sienna reminded her.

She smiled. "Yeah. I get your point. And just because Aaron and I hit it off doesn't mean that the boyfriend trade was good for anyone else."

Sienna knew Tracie was trying to be nice, letting her know that Mark's fling with Lily might not last. For all she knew, Mark was ready to return to her right now.

She reached up and played with some of the beads on the ends of her braids. Mark hadn't even said anything about her hairstyle, even though she'd had it done just for him. And if he really wanted her back, he would have called or come over. He hadn't even shown his face at lunch today. She sighed. "I bet Mark's fallen for Lily pretty hard. I guess that boyfriend trade worked out in their favor too. Or at least Lily's favor. You've seen her, with her little tank tops and her long hair she keeps flipping all over guys' faces. She's been flirting and shaking her body around Mark for a long time. She did practically everything but tie him up and drag him into her bedroom."

"I'm sorry, Sienna," Tracie said.

She shook her head. "Damn, I wish Lily had just stayed in one of her fantabulous European cities she's always raving about. First she took my place as lead singer in the band, and now she's taken my boyfriend."

"The last few days must have been so hard for you." Tracie reached across the table and put her hand over Sienna's.

"Well, I let everyone know how upset I was at practice. How embarrassing!"

"Don't worry about that. It happens to everyone. And you were in a hard spot," Tracie said.

Sienna found comfort talking to Tracie. Tracie might have lost her head by ditching Carter for Aaron, but she was still a considerate friend. "Amber Road means a lot to Mark," she told Tracie. "My dismal performance at rehearsal and my stupid walkout must have really upset him. Plus, it made me look like an idiot. You know I'm not like that. I've always been the one who helped Mark schedule practices and acted all professional and got to every rehearsal on time. Lily's the one who acted like she couldn't care less about Amber Road, showing up late, not memorizing the song lyrics. It's so unfair." She shook her head. "I bet once Mark gets to know Lily better, he'll realize what a selfish person she is. He'd better, anyway. When is it going to dawn on him that he made an awful mistake choosing her? If only I hadn't acted like a fool in practice."

"Now I feel guilty because I screwed up at practice too," Tracie admitted. "I was so distracted with Aaron there."

"I should have been more sympathetic to you," Sienna

said. "You tried to tell me you were getting frustrated with Carter, but I didn't listen until it was too late."

"Carter's a nice guy and everything, but he's not exciting like Aaron. Aaron makes me crazy." She giggled. "Look at this, Sienna." She lifted up her shirt and pushed down her pants a bit.

Sienna peered at Tracie's stomach, then choked a little on her sandwich. Tracie had pierced her belly button. A small diamond stuck out of it. What in the world had happened to her best friend?

"You like?" Tracie asked in a peppy voice to go along with the cheerleader smile she'd worn throughout most of lunch.

"I guess. Wow. I just never thought you'd get your navel pierced. I mean, you don't seem the type. I didn't even know you wanted to."

"I never thought I'd be dating Aaron Bouchet either. He thinks belly button jewelry is really hot," Tracie said, still holding up her shirt.

"You did that just for Aaron?" Sienna heard her own anger, but she couldn't stop herself. Besides, a good friend should tell a person the truth. "You put a hole through your stomach just to please a guy you've been dating all of five days?"

Tracie pushed her shirt over her belly button to cover the diamond, then crossed her arms.

Sienna crossed her arms too. "Geez, Tracie, you're going to Yale in the fall. You're supposed to be smart. Too smart to be throwing yourself at a boy."

Tracie looked at Sienna through narrowed eyes. "A boy? Aaron Bouchet is no boy. He's a *guy*, a *man*. Pleasing Aaron wasn't the entire reason I got my belly button pierced. I like my new navel jewelry. But, yeah. I want to make my guy happy. Sienna, there's nothing wrong with putting in some effort to satisfy your man."

What a dig! After Sienna had tried all through lunchtime to be understanding of Tracie and her silly infatuation for Aaron. *Could this lunch get any worse?* Sienna asked herself. At least Carter wasn't here to witness Tracie's ridiculous behavior. Where was he, anyway? She searched for him.

He was sitting with the water polo players, but staring at their table and frowning.

Sienna didn't know who was more miserable, Carter or her.

The bell rang and the girls stood up and gathered their things. Tracie said, "Aaron walks me to class a lot now. But since I don't see him, I'll go with you."

"How terribly generous of you to let me have your company when Aaron doesn't show." Sienna rolled her eyes.

"I didn't really mean it like that. Well, not exactly, anyway."

"I'm worried about you, Tracie," Sienna said as they walked toward their classes.

"Worried or jealous?"

"Huh? *Worried*, Tracie. You've been seeing Aaron less than a week, and it's like you've become a new person."

"A better person. Happier, anyway," Tracie said.

"I'm happy for you," Sienna lied.

Tracie shook her head. "Sure you are."

"I just don't see why you have to rush into things with him. For all you know, he might not like . . ." Sienna was going to say *needy girls*, but realized that was insulting. "He might get turned off by girls who get serious so quickly."

"It's kind of ironic, you giving me advice on guys."

Sienna glared at her friend. "What are you implying? Are you that cruel?"

"I'm sorry, but you're being cruel yourself. I think you may just be jealous because I hooked up with Aaron, and Lily hooked up with Mark, and you and Carter didn't hit it off."

"How do you know we didn't?" Sienna asked.

Tracie slowed down. "Did you?"

"No. I wouldn't steal your boyfriend," Sienna said. Tracie resumed her quick pace, so Sienna hurried to catch up. "Tracie, when I tell you my thoughts about Aaron, I'm only trying to help you, as a friend. And you're treating me like crap."

"You're not trying to help me. You're trying to ruin my happiness." Tracie arrived at French class. She quickly went in, even though there were still a few minutes before the bell.

Sienna's classroom was only two doors down. She stopped in the hallway and leaned against the wall. Her thoughts sped inside her head faster than a heavy metal song. Her best friend, the only person she felt she could count on these days, had been so rude to her. Tracie had basically said that Sienna didn't know how to keep a guy's interest. Not Mark's or Carter's either.

But Sienna had kept Mark's interest for a year, and planned to recapture it ASAP. As for Carter, she had purposefully avoided him, even though according to that stupid boy swap arrangement they were supposed to hook up. Sienna wondered why she even bothered to keep away from Carter when Tracie seemed to be totally over him. *What if Carter and I got together?* Sienna wondered.

No, she told herself. *Carter belongs with Tracie. And I belong with Mark. And the sooner things get back to the way they were—the way they're supposed to be—the better.*

fifteen

It was Cultural Sensitivity Week at school. Mark was all for being sensitive, and the "Show of Many Cultures" he was watching in the gym during fifth period sure beat one of Mr. Loring's calculus lectures. Everyone called him Mr. Boring, which was actually an understatement.

But the show in the gym wasn't that much more interesting. The first performance, a Native American dance, seemed to go on forever. Mark wished he could spend fifth period rehearsing with Amber Road instead. That would have been just as culturally sensitive. After all, Sienna was African American, George was Chinese American, Tracie's ancestors were German, Scottish, and something else that Mark forgot, Mark was Italian American, and Lily was in love with everything European.

He smiled as he thought about Lily. He wished she were

sitting next to him instead of Sienna, but Lily took a less challenging math class.

The drummer for the Native American thing wasn't very good. He kept varying the beat, which Mark didn't think was on purpose. If Amber Road played like that tomorrow at Waves, they'd never get asked back.

Mark had been nervous about the gig all week, but today he was near crazy with anxiety. Amber Road's last rehearsal had been a disaster. They needed to have another practice before tomorrow night.

He turned to Sienna, who had muttered "lame" a few minutes after the assembly began and proceeded to read a novel. "Could you come over after school today?" he asked her quietly.

She smiled and exclaimed, "Sure!"

Oh, no. He hoped Sienna didn't think this was a date. It would be cruel to lead her on. "I'm going to ask everyone in the band if they'll rehearse in my garage this afternoon."

"Good idea," she whispered, but her smile now seemed propped up.

"I'm going to look for Lily," he whispered.

Sienna didn't say anything.

"To ask her if she can make the rehearsal."

"Oh," she said, her smile completely gone.

"Do you know where Tracie is?"

"Nope." She scowled.

Had something happened between her and Tracie? Sienna was already upset with him and Lily. If things had gone bad between her and Tracie too, Mark worried that Sienna wouldn't want to stay in Amber Road. But now was not the time to talk about band relationships. For one thing, it was too noisy here. There was whooping from the Native American dancers, much whispering and talking in the gym bleachers, and shushes and muttered warnings from sour-faced teachers. Mark asked Sienna, "Will you help me look for the rest of the band so we can schedule a rehearsal today?"

Sienna nodded and said something that Mark couldn't hear because the Native American thing had ended and people were clapping.

Mark searched the bleachers until he saw Lily about thirty people away from him. Next to her was her brother, Aaron. Next to him was Tracie, of course. Aaron and Tracie seemed inseparable these days. Mark pointed them out to Sienna and whispered, "Let's go over there."

Clog dancers from Denmark or Sweden or one of those Nordic countries took the stage. The clog stomps were in sync and one of the dancers was a quite attractive blond woman; but the music, consisting of a wheezing accordion, was atrocious.

As Mr. Loring stared at the pretty clog dancer, Mark and Sienna left their seats and hurried toward Lily and Tracie. Mark thought he heard Loring call out to them, but he didn't look back.

As they got closer, Mark saw that Aaron had his hands all over Tracie as usual, and as usual she didn't seem to mind. Lily sat on Aaron's right, in an aisle seat. She waved when she saw Mark and Sienna.

"Is there any part of your body that Aaron hasn't felt up today?" Sienna asked Tracie.

Tracie laughed in response.

Mark perched on Lily's armrest. "I wonder what you would look like in a Heidi dress and clogs."

She snickered. "If that's your fantasy, I can try to make it happen."

"You look good in any kind of clothes," he said.

"And even better out of clothes." She winked.

"Whoa," Mark said. "I came over here to tell you something, but now I completely forgot."

Lily nestled her head on his chest. "I'm glad you came by."

"Let me remind you what you came here for," Sienna said behind him.

Damn. He could be so insensitive sometimes, flirting with Lily while Sienna stood next to him. Totally uncool.

"You're supposed to tell everyone we're having a band rehearsal today," Sienna said coldly.

"Yeah," Mark said. "Sorry. Can you guys make it? Lily? Tracie?"

"I'll be there," Lily said.

Tracie looked at Aaron. "Okay if I go?"

Mark had to force his jaw from hanging open. Tracie needed Aaron's permission to rehearse? That was just plain wrong.

Aaron nodded. "Sure you can go, babe."

"Okay, I'll be there," Tracie said. "I'm so nervous about performing at Waves, I could use all the practice I can get." She grimaced. "Oh, no. My class is leaving. The teacher warned us we'd have to skip out early so we can prepare for the AP test. I'd better go with them." She kissed Aaron on the cheek. But he drew her to him and rubbed her ass and whispered something that made her giggle.

What a sleazebag, Mark thought. And it was a little disconcerting that he was related to Lily.

As Tracie left, the clog dancers finished and a guy with a

huge sombrero, a glittery vest, and a guitar came onstage and started droning about the history of Mexican ballads.

"Could this show get any more lame?" Mark whispered to Lily.

She shook her head. "I doubt it. But at least you're here to take some of the pain away."

Aaron stood up. Was he going to follow Tracie out of the assembly? No. He climbed over his chair to the row behind them. Then he sat, or actually squatted, on Whitney Lowell's lap. Mark's jaw hung open now. "Let's go somewhere after school today," Aaron murmured to Whitney.

"Just us? What about Tracie? I've been seeing you two together all over school this week, all over *each other* this week too," Whitney said.

"She's not my girlfriend or anything," Aaron replied.

Sienna turned to him. "Does Tracie know that? Does she know you're all over other girls a minute after she leaves?"

Aaron shrugged. "What she doesn't know won't hurt her."

"You jerk." Sienna shook her head. "Lily, why don't you give your brother some lessons in human decency?"

Lily looked away. "I'm his sister, not his mother. Tracie can take care of herself."

Mark had never heard Lily sound so cold. "Tracie is my friend," he said. "Our friend. She's in our band, for God's sake."

He walked away, half hoping Lily would follow him.

After a few steps, he couldn't help turning around. Lily had stayed in her seat. She hadn't even turned her head to look at him. The only person who seemed to notice him was Sienna.

She stared at him with a hopeful expression. Or was he just imagining that?

He looked away, focusing his eyes on the show at the bottom of the bleachers, but his mind was busy elsewhere. Things were such a mess. He knew that Tracie, who was naturally so sensitive already, was going to get hurt badly by Aaron. Sienna was already hurt, and that was his fault. And he couldn't fix it because he couldn't resist Lily. The biggest performance of Amber Road's fledgling career was tomorrow night, and the band members' lives were in chaos.

The Mexican singer finished his boring song to tepid applause. Mark thought this assembly couldn't get any worse. Then a short, bald man in suspenders and shorts came out and started yodeling.

Mark rushed to the nearest exit.

sixteen

After school, Sienna hurried to Mark's house, hoping to spend time with him before the others got to the rehearsal. Mark had seemed angry at Lily today for defending Aaron's womanizing. He *should* be angry. No matter what Lily said, Aaron had no excuse for two-timing Tracie, their bandmate and friend.

Sure, Lily's exotic-looking and wild, but at least I have a heart, Sienna told herself. And so did Mark. A sweet guy like him wouldn't want a relationship with a selfish person like Lily. Mark finally saw her true colors today, and obviously didn't like them. When he had walked out on Lily at the assembly, Sienna had seen her opportunity. She hummed happily as she drove. She was about to reclaim her boyfriend.

As expected, there were no cars parked near Mark's house. Sienna had zipped out of school in order to be the first one here. She knocked on Mark's front door just in case; no one answered. So she returned to her Miata and reapplied her lipstick and combed her hair. She checked her reflection in the rearview mirror, keeping an eye out for her bandmates' cars.

Yes! Mark pulled up, alone. Sienna waved to him and he waved back. She would rescue him from Lily's clutches.

She met him at his car and they walked into the garage together. A few weeks ago, they would have greeted each other with a kiss, but at least today he smiled at her.

"While I was driving, I thought of this great line for a song," Mark said. "It sounded great in the car, anyway. Mind if I write it down before I forget?"

"Of course not. You have to meet your muse when she arrives," Sienna said, thinking that she was probably much more supportive than Lily was.

He took out his notebook and scribbled in it, then stared at what he wrote with a creased forehead.

"Need help?" Sienna asked him. They used to work on songs together a lot, though Mark did most of the creative writing.

"I'd love your help, Sienna."

And she loved hearing that.

"Let me play the melody I was thinking of, and you can tell me if it works, okay?" He stood in front of the keyboard and sang the line while he played.

This was just like old times, working closely together, just the two of them.

"So what do you think?"

Oops. She'd been so distracted by having Mark alone for a change, she forgot to listen to his song. "I'm not sure," she covered for herself. "Can you sing it once more?"

He did, and this time she concentrated on the song instead

of just Mark. He sang, "You race my pulse and flutter my heart, girl."

"It's a powerful lyric. Great first line," Sienna said. "I think the music is too fast for the words, though." She stood next to him at the keyboard, so close their thighs touched. She'd forgotten how much she liked his smell. It reminded her of new leather.

"Sienna?"

"Huh?"

"Did you hear what I just said?"

"Oh, sorry." Had he said something? She wished instead of talking they could just make out.

"I was wondering how the first line would sound with an extra note to slow it down." He played it.

"Much better," Sienna told him truthfully.

"Oh, and I just thought of the next line." He sang it for her. "You're not what the doctor ordered, but what my body craves."

Sienna forced herself to focus on the music rather than the familiar smell of him standing so close to her.

"It works," she said. "But I think you should add one more syllable in the first line to make the rhythm better."

"Yeah, you're right." He sang the two lines again, changing "girl" to "darling."

"Great. We work so well together." She leaned into him.

"Thanks. We do make a good songwriting team."

Not just songwriting team, Sienna thought. *A good team, period.* Today they weren't awkward with each other as they'd been since that stupid boy swap game. Now that Mark knew who Lily really was behind her tank tops and miniskirts, he probably appreciated Sienna more than ever. Maybe this temporary trading thing would actually prove good for their relationship in the long run. "Did I ever tell you how much I like your cologne?" Sienna asked.

Mark took a step away from her. "Cool! Tracie and George are here. And it looks like George found a new girl." He called out, "Glad you could make it!"

Sienna swallowed hard, then acted enthused to see her friends.

George had his arm around a Goth-looking girl with a bright white face, red lips, dyed black hair, and black clothes. Sienna didn't want to stare, but it appeared that the girl was wearing a black cape. Sienna instinctively put her hand on her neck, as if the girl would bite it if Sienna weren't careful. She noticed Tracie doing the same thing.

Sienna gave Tracie a little smile, and was relieved to see her smile back. She was glad to see that things were okay with her best friend after their argument, but she wished her bandmates hadn't come so quickly. She and Mark had been hitting it off. *It will be okay,* Sienna told herself. She was planning to stay in the garage with Mark after the rest of the band left. He would focus on her more after a successful rehearsal. Then she'd win him back.

After they greeted each other, Mark said, "I guess we should wait for Lily."

"As usual, Princess Lily is the last to arrive," Sienna couldn't help saying. "I guess she doesn't care that we're playing at Waves tomorrow night."

"Why don't we start without her? She can join in when she comes," Tracie said.

"*If* she comes," Sienna muttered. "I can fill in for Lily on lead vocals, you know."

"We know," Mark said.

Sienna smiled at him. "How about 'Touch Me, Thrill Me'?"

"Really?" Mark asked.

Sienna nodded. It was a powerful song and maybe she could seduce him with it. She used to sing it with subtlety. Lily played up the lyrics as if she were a dog in heat.

"Okay, I guess." Mark stared at the closed garage door. Was he worried Lily would find him enraptured by Sienna, or was he willing Lily to arrive and take over? Sienna could drive herself crazy wondering. She made herself concentrate on giving her all to the song.

They began. Sienna thought her soft, slow, quiet version sounded way better than Lily's raunchy way of performing the song. George drummed steadily, and Tracie played expert guitar. As Sienna sang, she remembered sitting in Mark's car just a few weeks ago, giggling while Mark sang, "Touch me, Sienna, thrill me." After the first verse, he had pulled over to the side of the road to make out with her. Then they had climbed into the backseat and made love, with Mark humming, "Touch me, thrill me." Soon they would have nights like that again, she just knew they would. As she sang and played her bass guitar, she stood over Mark at his keyboard.

Lily finally arrived near the close of the song. Sienna didn't mind. *Let her see how good we are together. Amber Road doesn't really need Lily, and neither does Mark.*

The song was great from beginning to end, and when they finished they gave each other high fives and George's date exclaimed, "You killed!"

Sienna got caught up in the excitement. Incredible music could do that to her. Being so close to Mark could do that to her even more. She reached over and hugged him tight, pressing her chest into his just as she used to do when they'd stand by her front door at the end of one of their dates. It felt incredible to be close to him again. They were so right together. She pushed her hips into him. She couldn't wait until they were alone.

But Mark edged away from her and eyed her with what appeared to be pity, his lips turned down in a slight frown. "I'm sorry, Sienna," he said. He might as well have shouted, *Get away from me!*

Lily walked over, stopping between Mark and her, as if to drive home the point that she had split them up.

Sienna stared past them and above them at a dark stain on the wall of the garage. Sensing that she was now the center of attention, she couldn't meet anyone's gaze for fear of bursting into tears. She had never felt so mortified in her life. How could she have made such a huge misjudgment about the way things stood between Mark and Lily? And how could Mark throw her off for Lily so easily? Had their entire relationship meant nothing to him? She contemplated running out of the garage, into her car, and rushing off. But that would just show everyone she was devastated. So instead, she remained frozen where she stood, wishing she'd never come to rehearsal today. In fact, she regretted ever auditioning for the band last year and ever dating Mark in the first place.

George tapped on his drum. "Dudes. We came here to rehearse, right?" he said. "Let's practice another song. If you guys don't get going, I'll tell knock-knock jokes until you start begging to get back to band rehearsal."

Good old George, always ready to distract the band when things got ugly. Things seemed to be getting uglier and uglier with Amber Road these days. Sienna looked at George's kind face, took a deep breath, and said, "Yes, let's rehearse.

Lily, now that you're here you can take over my spot." Unfortunately, Sienna's voice quivered. But at least she had been strong enough not to cry or run out of the garage.

"Thanks," Mark said.

Was he thanking George for getting them on track, or her for not causing a scene? Sienna dug her fingernails into her palm. Mark was lucky she wasn't shouting that he was an ass or that Lily was a tramp. It would serve him right if she did start a scene.

Tracie rubbed Sienna's back. "You okay?"

Sienna nodded, keeping her gaze on her guitar. She wasn't okay. She wasn't anywhere near okay. But she would pretend to be, and suffer through this rehearsal for the sake of Amber Road and any possible scrap of dignity she might have left.

seventeen

Backstage, Mark said, "The Hoodies are almost done with their set, and then we go onstage. You guys feeling good?"

"Like a frat boy in a sorority house," George said.

"I'm feeling great," Lily said.

Mark thought she looked great too. She wore a glittery white tank top and black leather miniskirt and sky-high heels that showed off her long, slim legs.

"I'm good too," Tracie said. Aaron stood behind her with his arms around her little waist.

Sienna nodded. "Ditto for me." But she didn't sound so good. Mark hoped her joy of performing would outweigh her discomfort in being around him and Lily.

The Hoodies' song ended and the group received scattered applause.

Mark hoped Amber Road would get a better reaction. "Let's go," he said, and they grabbed their instruments and rushed onstage.

A lot of their friends were in the audience, cheering. Mark wondered whether Carter would come to support Tracie, but didn't see him. It was probably all for the best because Aaron was here. The last thing they needed was to have two guys start fighting at Waves over a member of Amber Road. *Stop worrying,* Mark told himself. *Focus on the music.* "Let's rock all of San Diego!" he shouted.

"And the O.C. and L.A. too!" George added.

"And Tijuana and Ensenada!" Lily yelled. And they began. It was awesome. The audition last week was cool; but in Mark's eyes, actually performing at one of the best clubs in San Diego made Amber Road seem like a real, legitimate band.

And Amber Road was up to the challenge. They didn't make any mistakes, and they performed with fervor tonight. Mark totally felt the vibe. As he played keyboards, his fingers danced on the keys as if they knew just what to do without him even thinking about the notes. And his voice was its own instrument. When he harmonized with Lily and Sienna, it seemed as if the songs could not be performed by anyone but the three of them. They sang as if they had never felt a moment of tension between them. Everyone in Amber Road seemed really into the music and the scene and each other. They smiled at the audience and moved their bodies in sync with the magnificent sounds they created. They were totally *on.*

Again, Lily's singing was the standout. But there was a difference in her voice tonight. Mark had never heard her so passionate and intense. It was as if for the first time ever, she felt every note she sang deep in her soul. Mark felt more crazy about her than ever, and also more hopeful about the future of Amber Road than he'd ever felt before.

They played only twenty-five minutes because four bands were performing tonight, but Mark was both exhausted and exhilarated when their set was over. The applause lasted a long time, and Mark was thrilled to bow in front of a packed audience with the rest of the band.

He envisioned Amber in the first row, shouting and clapping harder than anyone. She was just as beautiful as before, her smile still toothy and very wide, her dark, long-lashed eyes as warm as ever. Then the vision grew cloudier and cloudier, until she disappeared. *Amber!* he called to her in his head. *Amber! We were awesome, weren't we? You heard us tonight, didn't you? I bet we did you proud.*

He rushed backstage, eager to celebrate with Lily and the others, knowing that they had surpassed all expectations for themselves. Sienna and Tracie stood together, arm in arm, as if they had never bickered this week. Mark said, "We were awesome. I'm so proud of you guys. We practiced hard, we made a great effort, and we totally rocked the house. I even saw Darby swaying from side to side. That was so cool! Amber Road is going places."

"We're going far." Lily hugged him.

"You amaze me," Mark told her. He threw his arms around her tightly. Mark was vaguely aware that they were surrounded by their bandmates, but it was so hard to resist Lily.

"I hate to interrupt you lovebirds."

Oh, man, that was Harry Darby's voice. Mark pulled away from Lily so he could give Darby his attention.

"Just wanted to congratulate you on a rad performance," the club manager said. "I want you back next Thursday. Deal?"

"You bet," Mark said. "I'm glad you liked our songs."

"Totally dug them, man. In fact, next week, keep impressing and don't be messing. We might have some managers and record producers in here to scope out a couple of the bands, ones that have been around the block longer than you kids. But I'm going to mention you to the suits. I'll tell them to stick around and listen to your sound too. They're always giving lip service about wanting fresh, raw talent."

"Awesome! Thanks, Mr. Darby," Mark said.

"No problemo. And thank you for doing that thing you do."

As soon as Darby left, Mark shouted, "Yes!" George gave him a high five, Lily jumped up and down, and Sienna and Tracie embraced again.

"We got our stuff together and brought it home tonight," Mark said. "Thank you, everyone, for working so hard and being so damn great."

"I'm glad it was such a success," Sienna said. "It's a school night, so I'd better get going."

Mark could tell she was hurt. As strong as Amber Road was onstage, it was weak offstage. He knew they had to fix their group dynamic, and he also knew that Sienna's unhappiness was completely his fault. "You all right, Sienna?" he asked her.

She nodded, but she didn't seem all right.

"Sienna," Lily said. "You did great tonight. Your bass and George's drums totally kept the whole band in rhythm." Then Lily took his hand. "You going to drive me home, Mark?"

Sienna's lip curled. She quickly turned away and left the greenroom without a word.

As the band leader, Mark felt he should follow her and try to make things better between them.

But Mark was also a guy with a beautiful girl holding his hand. Lily murmured, "We could, like, use the beach route and park by the ocean for a while."

Oh, man, he was so lucky. He moved closer to her and whispered, "I'd love to drive you home and stop at the beach." He brushed her silky hair from her eyes. "But I have to talk to Sienna. Will you wait in the club for me, Lily?"

"But, Mark," she protested.

He rushed out the door. Following Sienna wasn't just his duty as bandleader. He owed it to her. As his friend and former girlfriend, she deserved a lot more respect than he'd been showing her.

He raced through the parking lot. Sienna was already in her Miata, though she hadn't turned on the ignition yet. After he tapped on her window, she unlocked the car door for him. He got into the passenger seat, closed the door, and said, "I'm sorry."

"For what?" Her casual shrug was at odds with her choked voice.

"I'm sorry because you deserve better than me, better than how I've treated you this week."

She stared ahead, though there was nothing to see but a cement block and bushes at the edge of the lot, dimly illuminated under a gray lamppost.

"We had a great run, didn't we, Sienna?" he said awkwardly. He grinned as he remembered laughing with her on their last double date with Carter and Tracie. Then he remembered making love to her. She was a beautiful girl, in her own way.

"A great run? That's what you call our relationship? A week ago we were happily in love. At least I thought so. And now the year we spent together—working on the band, going out every weekend, making love—you reduce that to a great run? Did you come out to my car to insult me?"

"No, Sienna." He gazed at her, but she was still staring ahead. "I loved you. I hope you know that." He had thought he loved her, but he hadn't really known what true love was until he found Lily. "I still love you as a friend, Sienna. I want us to be friends always."

She shook her head. "Friends! You're asking me to be friends with you after you dump me for another girl in our band?"

Mark crossed his arms. "Sienna, I'm sorry. It just happened."

Sienna crossed her arms too. "I'm not your friend, Mark. I don't want to be. You can't hurt me like you did and then expect our friendship to last."

Mark took a deep breath. "I understand," he said. "But if we can't be friends right now, can we at least remain bandmates? You and I were always the ones who worked hardest for Amber Road."

"Yet you still made Lily lead singer." She uttered every word with anger.

He answered her calmly. "You're a great singer, Sienna. But I think you know Lily's voice is remarkable. You may not understand it, but that decision tore me up inside. I had to do what was best for Amber Road."

"You never even told me who Amber is, or was. I don't

even know if Amber is a real person, or even alive. I told you everything, but you kept that a secret."

Mark clenched his teeth. He hadn't felt ready to tell her. Maybe he should have realized that if he didn't feel close enough to Sienna after a year of dating her to talk to her about Amber, then Sienna was the wrong girl for him. He wasn't going to tell her about Amber now, not when she sat next to him in the car seething.

"You do what's best for the band and what's best for you, and never what's best for me," Sienna said.

"That's not completely true." He shook his head in the dark. "I came out here tonight because I thought it was best for you if we talked. Best for us, really."

"Maybe it's best if I leave the band."

"No, Sienna. Please don't. We need you on bass and we need your singing voice too, whether it's lead or not. Please stay."

She sighed.

"The band wouldn't be the same without you. We'd miss you so much. I'd miss you. Believe it or not, I do care about you."

"Well, you have a funny way of showing it."

He didn't respond. He knew there was no way he could convince her now that he cared about her, not after Sienna had just seen him holding hands with Lily.

They sat in the car in silence for a few minutes, until finally Sienna said, "I'll stay in Amber Road."

"Thank you." He didn't know what else to say.

"I'm not staying in the band for you. And certainly not for Lily. It's because I've put so much of myself into Amber Road. I worked so hard this past year, and now the band might have a chance to break out. And I'm staying for Tracie, and even for George. Not because of you, Mark. *Despite* you."

"I understand." He did. Sienna was a strong girl. Things would be rocky between Sienna and him, and between Sienna and Lily. But Mark suspected that Sienna would handle everything okay. Better than okay, actually. Probably with grace and fortitude. He loved her for that. But that feeling was a very different kind of love than the passionate love he felt for Lily.

"You can go now. Please," she told him.

He got out of the car without another word, then hurried back to Waves to find Lily.

eighteen

Tracie practically skipped out of the greenroom. This was one of the best nights of her life. She was happier now than when she'd opened Yale's acceptance letter. A lot happier, actually.

She had suffered much less stage fright tonight than ever before, and throughout the performance she'd felt as if being at Waves with Amber Road was exactly where she belonged. And even though she did exceptionally well in school, she had never had that feeling of exhilaration or absolute belonging in any of her classes. What really made the night special was knowing that Aaron was in the audience, rooting her on.

She didn't think she could be any happier, until Harry Darby asked the band to perform again next Thursday. Her life couldn't get any better than this, unless perhaps one of those producers or managers who were supposed to listen to them next week signed them on.

She sprung through the main room of Waves, searching for Aaron.

Oh, no. Carter sat at a table in front of her. Tracie's steps lost all their bounce. She hadn't officially broken up with him yet.

She knew she had to end things with him soon. She couldn't keep avoiding it. But she couldn't think of the right way to do it. She didn't know if there *was* a right way to do it. It was hard to imagine anything she could say that wouldn't hurt him deeply.

The truth was that breaking up with Carter was too painful to consider. She had loved him deeply and had imagined they'd be together forever. She still loved him, even now. Probably, she always would. She had never imagined falling for another guy. Breaking up with Carter would mean admitting to herself that her happily-ever-after dream of the two of them was over.

She couldn't do it.

She looked the other way, hoping Carter wouldn't notice her.

He did. "Tracie!" He stood up. "You were wonderful tonight."

She stopped walking. "Thank you," she said stiffly.

"Sit down. You must be tired." Carter apparently had been sitting by himself at the small table. He looked so alone at Waves, in his polo shirt and khakis and neatly combed blond hair, surrounded by people with tattoos and ripped jeans and hair dyed in loud colors.

Had he been here alone all night just to hear the band? Just to see her? She didn't have a watch on, but she was sure it was close to ten o'clock. Carter always tried to be in bed by ten on school nights.

And here she had been, ignoring Carter for the last week, totally focused on Amber Road and Aaron and herself. She had no intention of returning to Carter. As much as she hated to spoil a perfect night, she felt like she finally had to tell him things were over. She sat on the little stool across from him.

He reached out in an attempt to take her hand, but she put her hand on her lap. "Are you okay?" he asked.

"Of course I'm okay."

"Tracie, I don't want to neglect you. But I have. I haven't been giving you the priority you deserve."

What was he talking about? She didn't feel neglected by him. It was more like *she* had been neglecting *him*.

"But things are going to change with me," he continued. "Starting now. I don't always need to be in bed early on weeknights. And I don't have to go to every meeting for every group I'm in at school. I want to make you happy, Tracie. I want to be with you. I miss you."

Tracie sighed. The fact was that she was happier with Aaron now than she'd ever been with Carter. And she realized something shocking: In all honesty, she didn't miss Carter at all. God, she felt so shallow admitting that to herself.

He stared at her with wide, hopeful eyes. "What can I do to make things better between us? Let's do something crazy. We can go away this weekend. I'll drive us up to Lake Arrowhead. We can stay in my parents' cabin there, go hiking. Whatever you want, Tracie."

She put her hand over his, and he smiled. But she shook her head. "I should have told you sooner. It's not fair to you. We need to break up."

She felt his hand clench. "No, Tracie."

"I'm seeing Aaron Bouchet."

"No." He shook his head. "He's just a fling, part of a dumb game. You two don't have the history together that we have."

"We don't. And the years we went out were fantastic. I'm so glad we shared them. You meant a lot to me. You still mean a lot to me, Carter." She took her hand off his. "But the fact is, we need to move on. I . . . I've already moved on. I'm sorry."

Carter's face went pale and long, and his body drooped like a dying vine. "I thought that stupid trade was supposed to be for one night. All in fun, remember?"

She shrugged. "I thought so too at first."

"We've been together for years, Tracie."

"Maybe that's the problem."

"It hasn't been a problem for me."

She crossed her arms.

He continued arguing, as if he were at one of his debate competitions. "Listen. Aaron isn't even taking any AP classes. He's not in student government or Key Club like we are. You have nothing in common with him. I just don't understand it."

He was ruining his own case for himself. Not that he had a case. But knocking Aaron like that just made Tracie remember why she'd been unhappy with Carter the last few months. He was so into extracurricular activities and working hard at school and doing the right thing that he made little time for fun and spontaneity. "I don't fully understand my feelings for him either," she told Carter. "But I'm only seventeen. I want to see other people. And feelings aren't like a social studies test you can study for and conquer, or a math theorem you can disprove. They're just there. I don't know why I feel so strongly about Aaron, but I do. Just because he might not be as ambitious as you doesn't make him a bad boyfriend."

"Boyfriend?" Carter shook his head. Tracie restrained herself from nodding hers. "You've only been seeing him six days. Since Friday, right? And he's already your boyfriend?" Carter asked.

"We've gotten very close." That was an understatement. But Carter was hurt enough without hearing that Tracie and Aaron had been together almost every night this week. And if he found out what she and Aaron had done on the boat and in Aaron's car, he'd really be upset. A smile escaped from Tracie as she remembered her most recent makeout session with Aaron.

"Tracie, you're not going to sleep with him, are you?" Carter asked.

She didn't respond.

"After I waited all these years for you." He banged his fist on the table. "Do you know how much I wanted you? How much it killed me not to be able to make love to you? I was trying to respect you by not pressuring you for sex. But it turns out you have no respect for me at all."

God, she hadn't realized. She had always thought that keeping their virginities didn't bother Carter. Well, it was too late for them. The guy she really wanted to make love to now was Aaron.

"You're just going to jump into bed with him?" Carter asked.

"That's none of your business now," she said.

"You really know how to hurt a person, don't you?" Tracie had never heard him so choked up before.

She stood up. "I'm so sorry."

"How could you, Tracie?"

Tracie looked down at Carter, bent over the table as if he'd just been stabbed in the heart. She hated making him upset. But she also felt relieved that she'd finally told him they were over. There was nothing she could do now to make things okay for him. "You deserve someone better than me."

"But I want only you."

She shook her head and said, "I'm sorry," again. Then she walked away from him.

She stopped a few yards away. He sat with his folded arms on the table, his head slumped over them. She hated to leave him alone. If she kept walking, she knew that their relationship would end tonight, permanently.

On the other hand, she was eager to see Aaron, to celebrate Amber Road's success, to feel his hands caressing her, to hear him call her gorgeous. She kept walking away from Carter, in search of her new love, her new life.

It took her a few minutes to find Aaron because he was in the back of the room. Tracie wondered how well he'd been able to see Amber Road perform. On his table were plates of bar food—nachos and potato skins and fried mozzarella—and sitting with him were with the most popular people from school. Tracie recognized Whitney Lowell and some of her friends, a huge guy who played football, and a few baseball players. "Hey," Aaron said. "You were so hot tonight. Come here, gorgeous." He pointed to his lap.

She climbed on, and he wrapped his arms around her tightly. She felt completely right on Aaron's lap, as if she were made for it. Carter had never made her feel this way.

"Damn, Tracie," Aaron whispered. "The whole time you were onstage, all I could think about was how much I wanted to make love to you. Did I ever tell you you're the most gorgeous girl in the world?"

"All the time." She giggled. "But I don't mind."

"It's true, you know. And you played guitar like you were on fire. I'm on fire now." He kissed her neck.

"Get a room," one of the baseball players joked.

"You want to come over tonight? I cleaned my bedroom just in case you'd say yes." He stroked Tracie's thigh over her silk skirt. "My parents are on a business trip in Ohio. Lily's going to the beach with Mark."

Come over to his bedroom while his parents were away? Tracie knew what that meant. But was she ready for it? They had spent so much time together this week. Still, a week was barely any time to go out. Was Aaron sincere? Sienna thought he was a player.

"Please, Tracie." He cocked his head and stared at her with his charcoal eyes in a puppy-dog expression. "I need you to be with me."

He needed her. She needed him. And she needed to forget Carter's drawn face. "Let's go," she said.

In the car, Aaron took his hand off the steering wheel and put it on her right cheek, turning her face toward him.

God, he had a handsome profile too.

He stroked her neck, then slid his hand to her chest. "I can't wait to get you to my house."

"Me too. I mean, I can't wait for you to get to my house. I mean to get to your house." His hand was totally distracting her. "It'll be the first time I've seen it." As if she cared about looking at his house. The only room that interested her right now was his bedroom.

"First time at my house." He laughed. "You're going to love your first time." He put his hand on her thigh, this time under her skirt. For the rest of the ride to his house, his fingers caressed her legs, and reached higher, leaving her skirt bunched around her hips. He moved his hand down to her knee and squeezed it, then slowly up and all over her thigh again and up past that, then back down.

Tracie didn't speak, but her breaths came loud and labored. She could barely think of anything beyond how good she felt and where else she wanted his hand, where she wanted his body. On her, in her, soon.

Neither of them said a word until Aaron parked at the curb, kissed Tracie's forehead, and said, "Are you ready?"

"Ready?" she panted.

"Ready for anything?"

"Yeah," she managed to say as he reached down with both hands and squeezed the inside of her thighs.

He helped her out of his Porsche and they leaned against the passenger door for a few minutes. By the time they started walking up the driveway, Tracie's blouse was half unbuttoned and she was gripping Aaron's behind. She had to steady herself as she walked.

Tracie stood at the front door, her blouse completely open and her bra undone. She asked herself if she really should lose her virginity to a guy she had just started dating. She looked into his steely eyes to see if they were sincere.

Of course they were. They had to be. And they were smoldering hot, as was his tall, sinewy body that seemed to be composed of nothing but bones and rock-hard muscles. She couldn't wait to see him totally naked.

While he took the key out of his pocket and unlocked the door, she clamped her arms around his chest and pressed herself against him.

He put his arm over hers and laughed. He seemed calm and confident as a lion with his paw on young prey.

And Tracie felt as if she were loose in a dangerous, thrilling jungle. She clung to him, pulling up his shirt and kissing his broad chest while he opened the door. She kept her body wrapped in his as they walked into his house.

Aaron shut and locked the door behind him. "Thank God we're here," Tracie said as she unbuttoned his jeans.

He picked her up in his arms as if she weighed five pounds and carried her through the living room. Oh, God. Carter never did anything like that. "My bedroom's straight ahead," Aaron said.

"I can't wait that long." She could hardly believe what she was saying. She would never have said that to Carter. But she couldn't help herself. "Let's do it right here," she said.

So Aaron brought her to the living room couch and slowly drove her even crazier until she begged for him inside her.

Sienna had said the first time would be a letdown, that she would feel nothing but sore. Sienna had been wrong. *Obviously,* Tracie thought, *Sienna had never made love to a man like Aaron.* It hurt a little the first time but also brought Tracie a rush of amazement and joy. Aaron was ready for more a few minutes later, and by then Tracie felt only good things.

They finally went into Aaron's bedroom and made love one more time before they both lay still and sticky and spent in each other's arms. "Is that all you can do?" Tracie joked.

He smiled at that, and Tracie traced his perfect lips with her finger. Then she nestled her naked body closer to Aaron's and stared at his face on the pillow. His eyes were closed, so she studied his strong jaw, his rugged cheeks, the cleft in his chin. He was definitely the hottest guy she'd ever seen. She was so lucky to be with him.

Just before she fell asleep, Tracie told herself that the two best decisions she had ever made were her most recent ones: to agree to trade guys and to lose her virginity.

nineteen

Mark's mom ushered Lily into the house, her eyebrows raised higher than Mark had ever seen them.

That was understandable. His mom was used to Sienna, whom she liked a lot. Everyone liked Sienna—Mark's father, his little brothers, even his grandmother, whom Sienna had visited in the hospital after she'd broken her hip. Sienna was a sweet person. In fact, Mark still liked her a lot—as a friend.

But he sure was happy Lily was here. He hurried from the kitchen to greet her with a kiss on the cheek. Meanwhile, his mother stared at Lily's outfit, what there was of it, anyway. She wore a tiny, tight T-shirt, a short skirt, and platform shoes. Sienna wouldn't have been caught dead in those clothes. Too bad. That was one reason Sienna never looked as sexy as Lily.

"Sorry." Mark touched Lily's narrow shoulder. "I need

to finish loading the dishes and washing the pots and pans. Everyone in my family was talking so much, we didn't realize we were taking so long to eat dinner."

"Oh, that's nice. In France, dinner can go on for hours. I really miss that." She headed toward the kitchen. "Is the kitchen that way? I can help you clean up."

"You lived in France?" Mark's mom said as she walked with Mark and Lily.

"*Oui*. Before living in London and then here." Lily brought the pasta pot over to the sink.

"I spent a semester at the Sorbonne as an exchange student in college," his mom said. "It was wonderful." She and Lily reminisced about France as they helped clean the kitchen.

Mark sneaked glances at his girlfriend every so often as he stood at the sink. He liked her tonight more than ever, for not complaining about cleaning the kitchen and for getting along with his mom, while also looking incredibly hot in her sexy outfit.

After they finished clearing up, Mark and Lily went into the garage to practice. As the door closed behind them, Mark put his arms around Lily and kissed her.

Lily pulled away. "What if someone walks in on us? I don't want to upset your family. Your mom looked like she was about to faint when she saw me at the door."

Mark shrugged. "She just hadn't met you before. But I think you made a good impression on her."

"I hope so. I plan to spend a lot of time with you, so I want your family to be okay with that."

Mark felt a lump in his throat. Now he wanted to put his arms around her and kiss her more than ever. But he wanted to respect Lily's wishes too.

Lily sat in one of the folding chairs and crossed her long, slender legs. "Might as well work on band stuff. That's what I came here for, supposedly, remember?"

Mark sighed, then forced himself to stop staring at her legs. "Right. Band stuff."

"I was thinking of a new way of singing 'Right Beside Me.' Can I try it out for you?" Lily asked.

"I'd love to hear it."

She sang it much more slowly than Sienna used to do. Drawing out some of the notes made the song seem more poignant and showed off Lily's fantastic voice. It was an inspired rendition.

"I love it," Mark said. He felt like telling her, *I love you too,* but he didn't want to scare her. Instead, he said, "Remember the lyrics we came up with that night on the beach?"

"I remember everything about that night on the beach," Lily said. "I thought the song sounded really romantic, but maybe it was just because that whole night with you was really romantic."

"I'm dying here," Mark said. "Are you sure I can't take you in my arms and kiss you? It's Saturday. Weekends should be for fooling around."

She smiled. "Not with your family right outside the door."

"It was worth a shot. But can we take a rain check on that?"

"Definitely."

Mark took out the music he'd written and sang the lyrics. "What do you think?"

"It sounds like a great beginning," Lily said.

"So I should write more?" he asked.

"I'd love it if you did. And I'd sing it with total passion, just remembering you that night, looking at the sky, walking on the sand, swimming naked in the ocean."

He ached for her now. But he made himself behave, infusing the passion he had for Lily into creating the song. The next lines came easy for him. "I fell in love today, down at the beach in the sand. Don't ask me how. I just knew now. Nothing's gonna take our love away."

Lily said they were terrific.

"What did I ever do without you? You're my muse," he told her. "'Beautiful Girl' is your song."

She beamed at him. "If it's my song, I want it to be great." She sang a few lines: "If it's right, right now, why should I slow down? Don't let me touch the ground tonight."

They stood side by side at the keyboard, writing and singing and trying out different melodies. They finished quickly. When Lily sang "Beautiful Girl," Mark was left speechless. It was the best song he had ever written.

"You know what I really think is beautiful?" Lily asked. "Being with you. Whether it's walking along the ocean or working on our music together, or even cleaning with you in the kitchen. I love being with you. I love you."

Mark put his arm around her and closed his eyes to savor the moment. He doubted heaven itself could make him happier than he felt right now. "I love you too, Lily." Mark opened his eyes and looked into Lily's. Her eyes were more beautiful than the clearest blue sky on a spring day. "We can't declare our love for each other without a kiss," Mark said. He reached over, put his other arm around her, pressed his mouth on hers, and kissed her.

This time she opened her mouth and kissed him back. Soon their tongues and hands were all over each other. If his family caught him with Lily, so be it. Any embarrassment or punishment would be worth it. A minute later, everything—songwriting, Mark's family, the rest of the band—everything but Lily's mouth and body became a distant memory.

Someone knocked on the door connecting the house to the garage. Mark and Lily moved apart in a hurry, and each put their fingers through their mussed hair. Lily had to yank down her T-shirt. *At least we have all our clothes on,* Mark said to himself.

His mom opened the door. "How's the work going?" she asked in an even voice. She either didn't know they'd just been madly groping each other, or was okay with it. Whichever it was, Mark breathed easier.

"We just finished writing a great song." Lily pushed down her miniskirt.

"Oh, good. I came to tell you I'm going out. Mark's brother Kyle just told me he has to make a miniature log cabin for Boy Scouts tomorrow." She shook her head. "He's known about it for weeks and this is the first time I've heard about it. So I'm taking him to the art supply store. Then I'll swing by the karate studio and pick up Jay."

"I'd offer to help, Mrs. Carrelli, but we really need to rehearse," Lily said.

Mark's mom sighed. "Thanks, anyway. I wish my husband weren't on his fishing trip with his buddies. He's better at these craft projects than I am." She turned toward the house. "Okay, take care. If you're hungry, there's plenty of food to nosh on."

As soon as she left, Mark looked at his watch. They still had almost an hour before the rest of the band was due to arrive. He wondered if Lily would let him take off her shirt.

"Now that I've been in your house and met your mom," Lily said, "do you think you can tell me why you named the band Amber Road? Who is Amber? Is she really that great?

"Oh, Lily. I love you so much, but I'm not sure I'm ready to talk about her yet." He might cry if he did. He didn't want to be sad today. He'd been so happy with Lily.

"Fine." Lily sounded like it wasn't fine, though. She seemed hurt. "Let's work on another song, then. That's what we're supposed to be doing, right?"

Mark nodded. So much for making out with her. *Damn.* "Okay, let me get my notes. There are a few songs I started, but got stuck on. Maybe you can help me." He leaned down and riffled through a box on the floor of the garage that was filled with papers.

He heard the door leading to the house close again. When he looked up, Lily was gone. "Lily?" he called out. "Are you all right? You're not mad at me, are you?" *What did I do?* he asked himself. *Damn, damn, damn.* "Lily, where did you go?"

He walked to the door and opened it. One of Lily's platform shoes lay on the other side of the doorway. He didn't see Lily. A few yards ahead lay her other shoe. He picked up her shoes and kept walking.

Lily's T-shirt lay at the entrance to the living room. *Hot damn!* He rushed in. A yard away from her shirt, her little denim skirt was lying on the rug. Finally, next to the couch lay a lilac thong. And Lily herself—gorgeous, sexy, wild Lily—lay on the sofa wearing nothing but a grin. She was even more beautiful naked than he'd imagined all those times. "You still just want to write songs?" she asked.

In response, he ran over to her and ripped off his clothes as fast as he could.

twenty

"Your mom told me you were practicing," George said. "She didn't tell me you were practicing kissing."

They stopped kissing and turned around. George was holding hands with someone dressed like Princess Leia from *Star Wars,* with braids over her ears and a white dress that looked like a robe.

"Mark's a great teacher of the art of kissing. He's showing me some new techniques," Lily said.

Mark smiled. George could have seen a lot more than just kissing. After making love on the living room sofa and cuddling in each other's arms, he and Lily had gotten dressed and returned to the garage before his family and their bandmates were due to arrive. But he and Lily had started to make out again as soon as they closed the garage door.

"I have a girl of my own to kiss," George said. "Mark and Lily, meet Ashley."

Before they could say, *Nice to meet you,* the girl said, "Call me Leia, please. Or Princess Leia if you want to be more formal."

Mark covered his mouth so he wouldn't laugh, then gave Ashley/Leia a quick nod.

"She's auditioning tomorrow for a role in the new play *Star Wars, the Musical,*" George said. "She's been in Princess Leia–mode for over a week."

The rest of the band arrived soon after. Mark and Lily performed their new song and the group loved it. Though in Tracie's case, that wasn't saying much. She seemed so happy, she probably would have loved a rendition of "Ninety-nine Bottles of Beer on the Wall."

There was a lot to be excited about. Tonight was devoted to band promotion. First they made a podcast of two of their best songs, "Rock It Like a Rocket" and "Don't Leave." Then they decided "Beautiful Girl" was such a great new song that they recorded it on Mark's computer and added it to the podcast. They put the podcast online for people to download. The podcast also promoted their upcoming gig at Waves.

They worked hard. Luckily, Ashley/Leia turned out to be very knowledgeable about computers. She was helpful as long as everyone remembered to call her Princess Leia and not laugh when she said the Force was with her.

Mark was thrilled. The night had started off perfectly, writing an amazing song with Lily and making passionate love together, and then working with his friends in the band to promote Amber Road. "Listen, guys," he said. "With the podcast and the flyers we've been plastering all over the place, we might draw a big crowd at Waves on Thursday night. And remember that Harry Darby said there'd be record producers and band managers there. So our next performance at Waves could be our big break. Just five nights from tonight, our lives could completely change. We need to do a totally kickass set."

"You got it!" George banged on his drum.

Ashley/Leia flashed an imaginary lightsaber.

"We'll kill Thursday night!" Sienna shouted.

"Go us," Tracie yelled.

Everyone clapped.

Mark clapped so hard his hands hurt. He felt that Amber Road could go far. Everyone was working well together, and Lily was really focusing now on getting the most out of her amazing natural talent. The new song he and Lily had written tonight was an expression of their love for each other, so of course it turned out awesome. Mark hadn't been this happy since before he had lost Amber. He wished this night, with Lily and his friends and great music, could last forever.

twenty-one

"Have you been touring a nuclear reactor?" Sienna asked Tracie. They sat across from each other at Starbucks in the mall on a rainy Sunday afternoon.

"What?"

"You're positively glowing," Sienna said.

Tracie giggled. She'd been incredibly happy the last week and a half, but hadn't realized it was that obvious. Being with a totally hot guy who treated a girl like a princess would make anyone glow.

"Now your face is even redder."

Tracie looked down at her latte, but she couldn't hide her huge grin. "I spent almost the entire weekend at Aaron's house," she gushed. "His parents weren't home."

"Girl!" Sienna exclaimed. "But *your* parents were home. How did you get away with sleeping at a guy's house?"

"Remember, it's not just Aaron's house. It's Lily's too. My parents think Lily and I are bosom buddies now."

Sienna shook her head. "I bet Aaron is your bosom's buddy now."

"He's my bosom's best friend." She laughed.

An old woman at the next table glared at her.

"So, Tracie." Sienna lowered her voice. "I take it your virgin days are over?"

Tracie looked up and whispered to her friend, "And my virgin nights. After all those years being a good girl with Carter, I lost the Big *V* with Aaron Thursday night. We spent the past few days and nights making up for lost time." Just talking about it was making her hot. God, she loved making love.

"Well, judging from the smile taking up most of your face, I'd say you're one very satisfied customer," Sienna said.

"Very."

Sienna stared at her. "You used condoms, I hope?"

"I bet we'd make the cutest babies together," Tracie said.

"Are you nuts?" Sienna's voice had gotten so loud, the old woman at the next table and almost everyone else at Starbucks turned toward them.

"I meant we could create cute babies together in about a decade. Not now," Tracie said. "It's hard to rock out when your stomach is all swelled up."

"Not to mention go to Yale while taking care of a baby."

"Yeah, that too." Yale was the last thing on her mind these days. She didn't even want to think about being three thousand miles from Aaron. She couldn't picture herself getting on a plane to Connecticut, leaving the best thing that had ever happened to her. She might not even go to college at all.

"So you used condoms?" Sienna nagged.

"Of course. Lots and lots of them, actually." Her smile returned.

"Big condoms?" Sienna joked.

"Size extra-extra large."

Both girls cracked up.

"Perverts!" the old woman said. This made the girls laugh even harder.

When their laughter simmered down, Tracie said, "Hey, Sienna, anything to report in the old love life department?"

Sienna shook her head. "Absolutely nothing."

"I'm sorry," Tracie said. Sometimes she could be so insensitive—going on and on about her new boyfriend after Sienna had lost hers. Their friendship had been a lot easier when both she and Sienna had steady boyfriends.

"Ever since that night we traded guys, I'd been thinking Mark would come back to me. But it finally hit me that it's totally over between us, that he's with Lily now a hundred percent. That hurts." Sienna stood up. "I know just the medicine for the blues, though."

"Retail therapy?" Tracie asked.

"Right on, sister. Hot Topic first? Or maybe Bebe?"

"Let's take a walk on the wild side." Tracie got up too. "We're supposed to be buying outfits for our big performance Thursday night. We don't want to look like we dressed for school or something. We need to wow the audience. And hopefully the record producers and managers, if they show."

Sienna shook her head. "I'm not going to Frederick's of Hollywood."

"We don't have to dress like hos, but we shouldn't look like prep school students either. Aaron says I should show off my legs more. I was thinking of getting either supertight pants or a miniskirt. And I want them cut really low so I can show off my belly button jewelry."

"Wait a minute. Is this outfit for you to feel great at Waves on Thursday, or are you just trying to please Aaron?" Sienna asked.

Tracie shrugged. "Both, I guess." Sienna acted as if it were such a bad thing to want to make your guy happy. Aaron sure had pleased Tracie this weekend. There was nothing wrong with trying to please him too by dressing as sexy as he made her feel. "There's a new boutique store near Macy's," she told Sienna. "It's called Flambé. I heard Whitney Lowell talk it up at school, and you know how popular she is."

"Tracie, you used to dress for yourself, not to please a boy-friend or to be popular."

Tracie headed out of Starbucks. "Are you going to lecture me?"

Sienna followed her. "Sorry, Tracie, it's just that I care about you. I'm your friend."

"Okay," she said. "Just remember that it's good to shake things up every so often. Change isn't necessarily a bad thing."

"For me it is. Since Lily came along and shook things up with the band, I lost both my spot as lead singer and my boyfriend."

"I'm sorry." Tracie hugged her friend. But she couldn't help thinking how great her life had become lately. Aaron had shaken her up, and it had been a good thing. "But no matter how much everything else changes, we'll always be friends, Sienna. I hope so, anyway."

"We will be," Sienna said. "Okay, show me where this Flamboyant place is."

Tracie giggled. "Flambé. Not Flamboyant."

"Whatever," Sienna said. Tracie gave her credit for not rolling her eyes. She could tell she wanted to. But Sienna accompanied her to Flambé without complaint.

Tracie paused at the entrance of the store. She knew Flambé wouldn't exactly be Lands' End, but she hadn't expected the clothes to look this strange. With her fair coloring, she usually dressed in white or ivory or pastels. But most of the clothes here were black or red or weird metallic shades. A lot of the skirts were supershort. The others were ankle length and awfully narrow. The dresses were strange too. Some of them looked like shirts with a couple of extra inches added at the bottom. Others had asymmetrical holes cut from them in bizarre areas, as if someone had taken scissors to the fabric randomly. Frankly, Flambé's clothes scared her a little.

Sienna picked up a pair of tiny pants that had one red leg and one orange leg. "What planet are we on?"

"Don't be afraid of change," Tracie said, hoping to persuade not only Sienna but herself too.

Next, Sienna held up a dress that looked like a tight T-shirt with a strip of lace sewn on the bottom. "I'm worried if we appear at Waves wearing clothes from Flambé, the police will storm the stage and arrest us for public indecency."

"No, they won't."

"That was a joke," Sienna said.

But Tracie didn't laugh. Whitney had specifically recommended this place, and Aaron had said more than once that Whitney was hot. There must be something great about these clothes that Tracie just didn't recognize.

"I see they carry bras and underwear here too." Sienna was

holding up a thin halter top and matching microminiskirt. She sighed. "Let me know if you see anything decent."

Decent. Meaning not indecent. Tracie grimly sorted through racks of clothing. At least there were a lot of clothes in her size. In department stores, where she usually shopped, size threes could be hard to find.

"How about if we go to Nordie's after this and I'll look for something I can wear without either dying of laughter or dying of shame?" Sienna asked.

Sienna was starting to get on her nerves. "Fine," Tracie told her. "But I'm going to live a little and try on some of these clothes. Sometimes you just have to go for things in life that don't seem exactly safe at first." Like Aaron. If she hadn't agreed to go for it and swap guys that night at the beach, she'd probably still be with boring Carter now, wondering why she felt so miserable.

"I'll sit over there and wait for you." Sienna pointed to a red velvet ottoman near the front of the store.

Tracie picked out a few skirts and tops and dresses. They were peculiar, to say the least. But she remembered how Aaron had looked at Whitney in the cafeteria the other day, at her silver T-shirt dress that looked spray-painted on, with cutouts along her waist. Tracie had caught him licking his lips. He had said it was just because he was hungry. *Hungry for what?* Tracie wanted to ask, but didn't.

So she took the clothes into the dressing room and started trying them on.

She could barely get the first shirt over her chest. It was a lime-green thing that plunged in both the front and the back. She stared at herself in the mirror. She looked sexy, her curves accentuated, every detail of her lacy bra visible. Her ribs even showed up under the thin, see-through fabric of the cropped shirt. Everything about the shirt felt tight, but it seemed designed to fit like that. How could Tracie play the guitar if she could barely move her arms? She kept the shirt on while she tried on a tiny white miniskirt. She looked in the mirror and thought she resembled a hooker.

She was happy to take those clothes off. But the next thing she put on, a red dress with black lace at the hem and bodice, was even worse. She was not well endowed, but the little she had threatened to pop out of the lace on all sides. She couldn't imagine herself singing with abandon onstage while worrying she'd be flashing the audience at any moment.

"Holy crap!" Sienna exclaimed.

What was that? Tracie grabbed her purse, tried to adjust the dress, opened the door, and rushed out.

Sienna was still sitting on the velvet ottoman near the store entrance, but now she shared it with a bald, middle-aged man who stared at Tracie with wide eyes and his mouth half open. Gross.

"Are you okay?" Tracie asked her friend.

"I won't be if you buy that outfit. It's awful," Sienna said.

Tracie put her hands over her chest to cover herself up as best she could.

The lecherous man on the ottoman kept ogling her. He hardly even seemed to blink; he probably didn't want to miss anything.

"What was the 'holy crap' scream for?" Tracie asked her friend.

Sienna walked over and put her arm around her. "Oh, Tracie. Whitney just came in here."

"So?" Tracie said. "What's the big deal?"

"She was with Aaron," Sienna said. "He had his arm around her."

"You must be mistaken." Tracie shook her head. "It couldn't have been Whitney that you saw. If it really was Whitney, she would have come in and stayed a while. She told me herself she loves this place."

"She wanted to shop here, but Aaron refused to wait in the store while she tried on clothes." Sienna winced, as if she actually didn't want to bad-mouth Aaron. "He offered to buy her lunch at the food court instead."

"What?" Tracie felt her face tense, as if someone had sprayed it with starch.

Sienna nodded. "I'm just telling you what I heard."

There had to be an explanation. Aaron had held her for hours over the weekend. They'd made love at night and in the morning and the afternoon too. Just about two hours ago, she had been in his arms. He said she was the most gorgeous girl he'd ever seen. "Aaron and Whitney are just friends. Good friends," Tracie said.

She was already starting to feel better. There were probably a hundred valid explanations for what Sienna claimed to have seen. For one, Sienna had never respected Aaron. She likely saw him just as a handsome, confident guy. Sienna didn't understand what a great personality he had too. For instance, when they had watched *SpongeBob* in bed last night, Aaron had done funny imitations of all the characters. Sienna didn't know that Aaron was easily ticklish, or that he had a scar on his knee from being bitten by a dog—a chihuahua!—when he was a kid. Sienna was obviously still hurting so much after Mark left her that she couldn't see the good in anyone's relationship. And the fact that Aaron was Lily's brother didn't help matters.

Tracie told herself she had no reason to worry about Aaron; it was Sienna she should be concerned about. "Maybe he had his arm around Whitney because she was upset," Tracie said.

"She didn't look upset. She looked happy," Sienna pointed out.

"They're friends. They can comfort each other," Tracie said. "And what if that wasn't even him? You know how popular Whitney is. She probably hangs with lots of tall, cute guys. The person you saw could have even been her brother or something."

"Tracie," Sienna persisted. "Try to think logically about this."

"Me? I'm not the one jumping to conclusions. I know you're upset because everyone in the band except you is part of a couple now. You probably convinced yourself that was Aaron and Whitney because deep down you were hoping something like that would happen. Maybe it was Whitney with another guy. Or Aaron with—I don't know—his sister. Maybe he had his arm around his sister."

"For God's sake, I know what Lily looks like," Sienna said. "And Aaron too. Instead of admitting that your boyfriend might be two-timing you, you start attacking me."

"Well, I don't believe it."

"Listen," Sienna said. "I didn't want to say anything to you before in case Aaron and Whitney really were just friends, but at that stupid cultural sensitivity assembly last week, Aaron was practically sitting on Whitney's lap and making plans to get together with her."

"Yeah. They're friends. That's all. Aaron and I have something different. Special. We made love. We spent the weekend together." Tracie put her hands on her hips.

The bodice of the little dress fell down. "Darn it!" She pulled up the dress, but that just made its short skirt move up, giving Sienna and the lech on the ottoman a view of her underwear. "I hate this stupid store Whitney told me I had to shop at! I'm putting my normal clothes back on and I'm getting out of here."

She hurried into the dressing room and changed back into her own clothes. What a relief. She didn't want to spend another minute here, especially with her jealous so-called friend. She'd rather be home, plopped on her bed reading a romance novel or taking a nap. After the wild weekend with Aaron, she needed some sleep. Plus, she hadn't done any homework this week. She was far behind in school for the first time in her life.

Once Tracie was dressed again, in her own pink cotton blouse and comfortable faded jeans, she rushed out of the dressing room. "Let's go," she told Sienna. "You still want to shop at other stores? Personally, I'd rather leave the mall altogether. I'm just not in the mood for shopping."

"What about Aaron?" Sienna asked.

"What about him?"

"Don't you want to make sure nothing fishy's going on?"

God, Sienna just wouldn't let up. "Believe me, that wasn't him. He'd never put his arm around another girl. You don't know him like I do."

"Let's go to the food court and find out."

Tracie forced herself to shrug as if she had complete confidence that Aaron wasn't with Whitney. "Fine, we'll go to the food court. I'm kind of thirsty anyway." Sienna would probably point out a couple who barely resembled either Aaron or

Whitney. Then Tracie could say *I told you so* and Sienna would stop making false accusations about Aaron.

What if it was them, though? Tracie put that thought right out of her head. Or tried to, anyway. She was walking so slowly, almost as if she wanted to give them time to leave. No! That wasn't it! It wasn't them! Tracie was just tired from lack of sleep this weekend and from trying on those horrible, tight clothes.

She spotted them sitting at a table right by the entrance to the food court. Even if she hadn't been looking for Whitney and Aaron, they would have been hard to miss. Whitney was on Aaron's lap, facing him—the same position Tracie had been in a few nights ago. They were kissing. His hands—his large, gentle hands that had just caressed Tracie this morning—were on her butt, massaging it as they kissed. It was so tacky, so cheap, so absolutely disgusting.

"I'm sorry, Tracie," Sienna said next to her.

She didn't speak. She didn't move. She stared at them, the traitors, as she stood just a few yards away, in front of a trash can that smelled almost as rotten as she felt.

"I just thought you should know." Sienna touched her arm.

Tracie flinched and took a step away.

"Tracie, you okay?"

Okay? Okay? Of course she wasn't okay. How could she be?

And then Aaron saw her. His hands flew off Whitney and he jerked his mouth up and back to untangle himself from the kiss.

Whitney turned to look at Tracie. Tracie thought she saw her smirk.

"I want to kill myself," Tracie murmured to Sienna.

"Oh, no. Kill Aaron, not yourself."

"How could he?"

"Because he's a bastard, that's how," Sienna said. "I wouldn't mind killing him myself."

Aaron left Whitney on the bench to walk over to them. Whitney pulled a compact out of her purse and calmly powdered her cheeks as if it were perfectly fine to be caught kissing someone else's boyfriend. Tracie had never much liked her, but now she hated her—her heavily foundationed face and big red lips and dyed blond hair and the smug expression she always wore.

"I'm sorry," Aaron told Tracie.

"Do you not possess even a shred of decency?" Sienna asked him.

He frowned and hung his head.

Tracie couldn't help thinking how handsome he looked, how vulnerable, almost like a little boy, with his face flushed and his hair mussed. *You're such a fool,* she lectured herself. *He probably looks like that now because Whitney ran her fingers through his hair and did God knows what else to get his face flushed. Or maybe his face turned red as soon as he realized he'd been caught with Whitney. He's no good,* Tracie told herself.

"I'll let you two talk," Sienna said. Then she whispered to Tracie, "Break up with him. You deserve someone a lot better."

Carter. The better "someone" had to be Carter. That's what Sienna must be thinking. No one had forgiven Tracie for dropping Carter for Aaron. But Carter had never made her as excited as Aaron did. And it wasn't just the sex. It was also the crazy things she did with Aaron—drinking with him, hanging out on the yacht, getting her belly button pierced for him, even though the stud hurt her sometimes and Aaron hadn't been as happy about it as she'd hoped.

But Carter would never make out with another girl while they were dating. Only Aaron had stooped that low. "How could you do this to me?" she asked him.

"I said I was sorry, babe. I had no idea you'd be at the mall."

As if the only thing wrong were that he'd been caught! "I thought we were a couple," she said.

"You haven't been exactly faithful either. You're the one who's had a boyfriend most of the time we were going out."

She supposed it wasn't just Aaron who had stooped low. She had cheated on Carter too. But that was different, sort of.

"And it's not like we're engaged or anything," Aaron said.

"I thought we were . . ." She stopped herself from saying *in love*. After all, Aaron had never said he loved her. Not in so many words, anyway. She hadn't told him either, because she didn't want to scare him off. But she loved him, deeply, completely. "I thought we were . . . we were a couple," she told him now.

"We were—uh—are. You're the most gorgeous girl I've ever known. You are so special to me, Tracie. I'm crazy about you."

She felt herself smiling.

No! Sienna would murder her if she caved so easily. But Aaron had just said that they were a couple, that she was gorgeous and special, that he was crazy about her. Saying you were crazy about a person was like admitting you were in love—pretty much, anyway. Didn't that deserve at least a little smile? Besides, she couldn't help the expressions that formed on her face. She couldn't fight the fact that his mere presence made her happy.

He put his arms around her and drew her close.

Tracie wondered if Whitney was watching. She hoped so. She wanted her to see that despite Whitney's slutty clothes and attempts to nab another girl's boyfriend, Aaron still picked Tracie over her.

Aaron kissed the top of her hair. He was so tall and strong. His arms seemed like they were made especially to hold her. She wanted to smell his now familiar, musky aroma. She sniffed in. Ugh. He smelled like flowers.

It was probably from Whitney's perfume. She stopped smiling. What was she doing in his arms after he'd just sneaked around on her? "How could you cheat on me?" she asked him.

"I'm really sorry." His voice was soft, like he really was sorry. "It just kind of happened. We went to get something to eat and then she suddenly kissed me, right in the food court."

Tracie didn't want to hear the details, but she felt compelled to. She prodded him. "You kissed Whitney back."

He stared down at her with his searing eyes. "You know you're my special girl. I hope you know how special you are, anyway. We just had the best weekend together. We can't deny that."

"It was perfect. I thought so, anyway. So why didn't you push Whitney away when she tried to kiss you?"

"Listen, Tracie. It's hard to give you my all when I know you're moving cross-country. By next fall, you'll be at Harvard."

"Yale," Tracie corrected him.

"Right. Whatever. It's on the other side of the country. I can't commit to a girl who's planning on leaving me."

He made it sound as if she were moving just to get away from him. "I'm not leaving *you* per se," she told him. *Per se.*

Why did she have to use that term? He hated those "hoity-toity expressions," as he called them. She tried again. "I'm not leaving because of you. I just want the best education."

"I know, Tracie. But you'll still be gone."

She buried her head in Aaron's great chest. She hadn't thought about her plans from Aaron's perspective. *The poor guy must feel like he's not a priority in my life,* she told herself. There are plenty of good schools in Southern California. But she had chosen one on the other side of the country.

"I love holding you like this," Aaron murmured. His hands massaged her back, then drifted down to her bottom and patted it.

God, he managed to turn her on even while they were fully clothed in the middle of a mall.

"I'm really sorry about Whitney."

How could she even think of leaving him? He had said he was sorry, but *she* actually owed *him* an apology. She lifted up her head so she could look him in the eye. "Listen, Aaron. I don't have to go to Yale. There's probably still time to apply to other schools. UC San Diego would give me a great education and it would be a lot cheaper too. And even if I went to UCLA or Pomona, they're only a couple hours away. Then I'd never have to leave you, Aaron." As she spoke, it all sounded so doable and so exciting. "We could even live together next year, in a little apartment near campus, and we could be with each other every night. Oh, can you imagine!"

"Whoa." He stepped back. "I like you a lot, Tracie, but we've only been seeing each other a little more than a week. Slow down. I don't even really know if I want a girlfriend right now."

She nodded, because if she tried to speak she might burst into tears.

"I mean, I totally still want to see you, but I'm not ready to move in with you. Next thing you know, you'll want to pick out engagement rings." Then he laughed, like that was so funny. Imagine, two people who had been sleeping together and who were supposed to be crazy about each other, might want to get married. Ha ha. What a riot. Tracie blinked back tears.

He glanced in the direction of the food court. "Whitney's been waiting for me all this time." She was still at the table, but now with an iPod and headphones and a soda in front of her. "Don't worry, I'll resist her advances if she tries anything else. She can get pretty skanky." He patted Tracie's bottom again. "You want to get together again next weekend? My parents will be home, but we could go for a ride in my car. Or to your house if your parents go out."

"I'll see you Thursday, right? You remember we're performing at Waves? You said you'd come to hear us." *I really need you to be there for me,* Tracie wanted to say but didn't.

"Yeah, sure, I'll be there. My sister's in the band too, you know." Then he kissed her, hard, on the mouth.

She couldn't resist even if she'd wanted to. She kissed him back.

Then Aaron rejoined Whitney, and Tracie walked over to Sienna, who was standing nearby with her arms crossed.

twenty-two

Mark looked at his watch. It was already ten o'clock and they hadn't gone onstage yet. Amber Road would be the last band playing at Waves tonight. At least they weren't the first band performing, before a lot of people even got to the club. But the audience would be tired by the time they came on. To get their interest, Amber Road would really have to blow them away.

The club was packed. A lot of Mark's friends from the school orchestra were here, some probably with dreams of being in a band themselves. George's schoolmates showed up in big groups too. Sienna and Tracie had lots of supporters also. Even the AP class crowd came, many at their first live concert ever. Lily, on the other hand, brought kids who seemed to practically live for rock music, looking the wild band groupie part with piercings, dyed hair, skintight jeans or miniskirts, many of them smelling like cigarettes or pot. Everyone, no matter their background, seemed excited to be at Waves, eager to cheer on Amber Road during its big night.

Even Carter had been kind enough to come. Dating Tracie all those years, he had become close to the other band members. He walked over to their table and said he was rooting for them. Mark still wondered how in the world Tracie could have dumped such a nice guy for the arrogant Aaron.

And Aaron wasn't even here. So much for his grandstanding to Tracie a few weeks ago about never leaving a gorgeous girl like her alone. This was a problem. Mark didn't give a rat's ass about the guy. He seemed like a jerk. But Tracie had spent the night searching for him with no luck. She looked as if she could burst into tears at any moment. Mark wished she'd focus on Amber Road instead of on her absent boyfriend.

Mark checked his watch again. 10:01. They'd be on soon. The closer it got to their turn, the faster his heart beat. How could he sing tonight when he could barely breathe? Their songs weren't meant for trembling voices. No songs were meant for trembling voices.

Relax, he told himself. *You've done this before. The first time we were here we totally rocked.* But his heart refused to stop racing. Tonight was different. Harry Darby had said record producers and important band managers might be in the audience.

Mark studied the crowd. What did these producers and managers look like anyway? They were probably at least a decade older than him. But what else? Would they have notepads out to record their impressions of the bands? Cell phones so they could call their studios? Did they have business cards in their hands, ready to offer them to people they liked? Mark had no clue.

He gave up searching for them and turned his attention to his friends in Amber Road. They weren't exactly a calming influence. Tracie kept biting her lip and looking for Aaron, Sienna played with the beads at the ends of her braids, and Lily talked too much, which Mark had come to realize was a sign of nerves. Lily would never admit to feeling anxious, but Mark knew her well enough now to know when she did. Even George, usually so cool, kept tapping his finger on their little table at the club. But maybe that was just his way of keeping rhythm with the band onstage. Mark hoped everyone's edginess was due more to excitement than fear, as if they anticipated an exhilarating roller-coaster ride rather than a horrible trip to the dentist. He looked at his watch again. 10:04. He sighed.

Tracie tapped him on the shoulder. Her eyes were wide and her face almost white, unfortunately looking as if she were in the waiting room of a dental office. "I don't think I can go onstage without Aaron in the audience." Her voice quivered. "He's been there for me the last two times at Waves. I need him."

Oh, man. As if Mark didn't have enough to worry about. "Tracie, Aaron might actually be in the club. There's lots of people here. Maybe you just didn't see him."

"I've been searching everywhere for him. He's definitely not here. And he promised he'd come tonight." She bit her lip again.

"You'll do great on your own." He tried to sound calm. The last thing she needed was to hear panic in his voice. "Carter's here. He can support you."

"Carter." She said his name as if it repulsed her. "I need Aaron. Only him."

"But Amber Road needs *you*, Tracie. You can't let us down tonight. And Aaron can't be here for every performance. One day we might even go on tour, and you'd have to leave him behind then."

"No. I could never leave him behind."

For God's sake. He grabbed her hand. "Tracie. I want this opportunity so bad. We all do. I know you do too. Try to forget about Aaron while we're onstage, and just play your best."

She nodded, without any conviction it seemed.

Helium exited the stage to tepid applause. Mark thought they were full of hot air.

Mark whispered, "Please, Tracie, this means everything to me." Then he pulled her onstage with him.

Amber Road took their places and Mark went to the microphone. "Thanks for coming out, everybody. We're Amber Road."

The audience clapped and the band started its first song, "School Bites after Being Out All Night." As soon as they began singing and playing, all their anxiety seemed to disappear, or rather transform into passion and power. Mark looked over at Tracie. She was smiling and playing the guitar as if nothing mattered but the music. That was how Mark felt too, as if the music and lyrics were real, live beings flooding his heart. Once the members of Amber Road felt the vibe, they could relax and truly have a good time and rock out with the songs. *This,* Mark thought, *this vibe, this energy is what sets apart a good band from a great one. And we are great.*

The audience seemed to sense it too, becoming infected with Amber Road's enthusiastic spirit. The applause was huge for the first song. By the time the band started its second number, people crowded the small dance floor to celebrate the massive, awesome experience.

Mark and Lily performed their new duet, the slow and stunning "Beautiful Girl." No one in the audience made a sound, as if they were totally focused on the magic and beauty of the song. Some of them might have been envisioning their own beautiful lovers, past, present, and future. By the end of the song, the members of Amber Road seemed hot and sweaty and exhausted, and as if they couldn't keep smiles off their faces. Their schoolmates seemed to forget they were in the audience to support their friends. Instead, they just got caught up hearing a rockin' band and loving it.

Carter started a chant of "More, more, more," that caught on in about three seconds and swept the club and seemed to go on forever.

Their next song was "Kiss Me." It started off great, for about twenty seconds. Then Mark saw Aaron—on the dance floor with Whitney Lowell. He held her so close Mark could see only the back of her, the back of her extremely tight, very short dress and stiletto heels, and her round ass, on which Aaron's large hands were firmly planted.

Please don't let Tracie notice Aaron and Whitney, he prayed, though he knew God had better things to do than interfere in people's love lives. Mark braved a glance at Tracie. She obviously had seen Aaron and Whitney. She stood onstage, her hands frozen on her guitar, her body still, her head not moving, her eyes fixed on the vulgar couple on the dance floor.

Mark glared at them. How could Aaron do this to Tracie, to Amber Road, to Mark? It was rotten enough to cheat on Tracie. But it was ten times worse to bring a girl to Tracie's big performance on the biggest night of Amber Road's fledgling career, and to grope that girl a few yards away from them.

Mark shook his head and returned his attention to the stage. The band had been playing spectacularly up until this point. Now Tracie was worthless, he was too tense to focus on the music, and everyone just sounded off.

He wasn't sure what to do about Tracie. It was hard to think and play the keyboard and sing at the same time, especially while knowing that the future of Amber Road was about to become history.

Sienna started moving toward Tracie. They were best friends. Maybe Sienna could help her. But she also had to sing and play guitar, and how much use could she be while onstage in front of a huge audience? "Tracie!" she shouted.

Tracie had set down her guitar and was rushing off the stage, straight to the dance floor.

Mark tried to keep playing and singing, but his hands were like bricks on the keyboard and his voice did more squeaking than singing.

Tracie ran to Aaron and screamed, "You bastard!"

Aaron stopped dancing with Whitney. But he still had his arms tight around her.

"I hate you!" Tracie screamed at him, and threw herself on his back.

Whitney hurried off the dance floor and into the crowd.

Mark and Sienna rushed to Tracie and pulled her off Aaron.

Aaron shook his head and followed Whitney.

"Bastard! Bastard!" Tracie screamed after him.

Sienna put her arm around her friend as best she could. "Oh, honey, are you okay?" she asked her.

"No!" she screamed. "No, I'm not okay!"

Mark heard George beating the drums, probably hoping to drown out the crazy noises on the dance floor.

"Please, Tracie, calm down," Mark begged her in a loud whisper. "You're making the entire band look bad."

"That's all you care about, isn't it? Amber Road," she accused him. "You don't care that my heart's just been ripped apart."

"Oh, Tracie. That Aaron's such an ass," Sienna said. "He doesn't deserve you."

"I hate him!" she screamed. "And Whitney too. And I hate all the pressures of being in this band. It used to be fun, but now it's all about making it big, and Mark's grand ambitions, and . . . I hate everything! I hate myself! I—" She was wracked with sobs and couldn't continue. Instead, she ran away, off the dance floor, through the audience, and out of the club.

George said into the microphone, "Sorry about that," and he and Lily joined Mark and Sienna offstage.

After all their practice and songwriting efforts and auditions and attempts at promotion, Tracie had singlehandedly blown any chance Amber Road had for success. Mark felt like sobbing himself.

twenty-three

"Thanks for coming," Mark said. The others nodded. Lily, George, Sienna, and Mark were gathered in his garage, but today there was no band rehearsal. They were here, after school on Friday, sitting on folding chairs in a small circle, to talk about Tracie.

Mark sighed. "We might as well put it on the table. Tracie wrecked a lot of things for us last night, things we'd all worked hard for, things we'd been hoping for." He felt his throat tighten, so he paused before continuing. "Let's face it. She ruined our chance to keep playing at Waves, maybe even headlining there one day if we got lucky."

"Did Harry Darby say we couldn't come back?" Sienna asked.

Mark shook his head. "He didn't need to say anything. It's obvious. We totally messed up. And there was the possibility that a manager or record producer in the audience would have wanted to take us on." His voice had been getting louder and he felt like screaming, so he paused again and swallowed hard. "She made us look like amateurs even in front of our friends."

"We were on a roll until last night when Tracie went crazy," Lily said, next to him.

"But it's not like she did it on purpose," Sienna said. "I mean, your brother really hurt her."

"My brother." Lily crossed her arms. "As if *I* told him to bring Whitney Lowell to Waves."

"If only he'd brought a few extra girls, especially girls who are into long-haired Asian drummers," George said.

No one laughed.

"So what should we do about Tracie?" Mark asked. Sometimes he hated being the bandleader. He had to make hard decisions, and he knew he'd be blamed by anyone unhappy with them. If Tracie ever found out they were meeting behind her back to discuss her situation, she'd be beside herself. But it had to be done.

"What Tracie needs right now is sympathy and comfort. Besides being in Amber Road with us, she's our friend, remember?" Sienna said.

"We can comfort her and be friends with her without having to be in the same band with her," Lily said. "You all were there last night. She was completely out of control. What if she does something like this again?"

Sienna shook her head. "She won't. I don't know what kicking her out of the band would do to her emotionally right now, but with her fragile state it could really be dangerous. Anyway, what ever happened to loyalty to a good friend?"

Mark didn't know what to do. He agreed with Lily, that Tracie was dragging everyone down with her; but he also understood Sienna's argument that they were friends first, bandmates second. The two girls sat opposite each other, both literally and figuratively. And Mark felt caught in the middle.

"Since you're all about loyalty, Sienna, don't you think it was disloyal of Tracie to humiliate us in the middle of our set?" Lily asked.

"I hate to point this out." George sounded somber for once. "But Harry Darby might let us play at Waves again if Tracie weren't in the group anymore."

Mark hadn't thought of that. Maybe there was hope for Amber Road after all. But he also wondered if he'd even *want* to be in a band that kicked out one of its members when she had personal difficulties.

Sienna folded her arms. "Tracie's my best friend. If you guys force her out of Amber Road, I'm not sure I could stay in the band either."

Mark patted her shoulder. "She couldn't ask for a better friend than you, Sienna."

"That's what friends do," Sienna said, glancing at Lily. "I'll talk to Tracie. She just needs to forget about Aaron. Ever since she started seeing him, she hasn't been herself."

"Don't blame all of Tracie's dramatics on my brother, okay?" Lily said.

Mark realized this situation must be especially hard on Lily. How could such a nice girl like her have such a heartless brother?

"Damn," Sienna said. "Everything got so hard and complicated after the Waves audition and the . . ." Mark assumed she was going to say *boyfriend trade*. She didn't finish the sentence.

"We weren't always so serious about the future of Amber Road. Remember when we just liked to hang out together and make good music? We used to play high school dances just for the hell of it."

"We still can." George leaned forward. "There are tons of schools around here."

"Carter's heading the committee to plan our school's spring dance," Sienna said. "I'll ask them if they want us to play."

"And there are other clubs besides Waves, of course," George said.

"We don't need Waves. We just need each other." Sienna sounded more hopeful than she'd seemed in a long time.

But what about Lily? She had seemed opposed to keeping Tracie in Amber Road. Mark put his hand on her knee. "You think we should keep Tracie in the band? Even if that means giving up any shot of returning to Waves? We could slow down and play at high schools and other places just for fun, like we used to do."

"That's okay by me," Lily said. "I never liked being pressured to practice so much and to be exactly on time for rehearsals and stuff."

Mark admitted to himself that he'd pressured Lily too much, pressured everyone too much. Maybe if he hadn't made such a big deal about the future of Amber Road, Tracie wouldn't have been so anxious and the whole scene at Waves on Thursday wouldn't have happened. They had to keep Tracie in the band. Otherwise, he'd never forgive himself.

He turned to George. "So you don't mind taking a step back and playing at school dances?"

"Do I want to perform in front of hundreds of girls my age

who have a thing for rockers and are in the mood to party? Bring it on, dude," George said.

Mark cracked a smile for the first time since Tracie had made the scene at Waves. "We probably won't get paid, and high school gyms won't be as exciting as clubs like Waves; but we'll get to play music together. That's the most important thing," Mark said. "So you guys want to keep Tracie in the band?"

"Definitely," Sienna said.

"I just wish she'd jump on *my* back next time," George said. "I've had a kink in it for almost a week." This time everyone laughed.

"I'm willing to give her one more chance," Lily said.

"Me too," Mark said. Amber herself would choose kindness toward a friend over fame, he thought. "So it's settled. Tracie's still in Amber Road. I just hope she can pull herself together."

twenty-four

Tracie couldn't believe how understanding Sienna was being. After all, Tracie had totally embarrassed herself and destroyed Amber Road's reputation at the same time. Yet Sienna was goofing off in Tracie's bedroom today, polishing her toenails while Tracie leafed through *Rolling Stone* magazine, just like old times. "I'd forgotten how cool it is to hang with you," Tracie said.

Sienna smiled. "Yeah, this is nice. I know you were gaga over Aaron, but a girl has to make time for her friends too."

Tracie saw a picture of a tall, dark-haired rocker in *Rolling Stone* who reminded her of Aaron, except Aaron was better looking. She sighed. Everything reminded her of Aaron these days, and Aaron was better looking than everyone. "Believe me," she told Sienna. "If I had known how awful Aaron was, I never would have dumped Carter for him."

Sienna shook her head. "Damn, that boy's a player."

Tracie turned the page of the magazine. The picture of the rock group posed on a yacht reminded her of the time she sneaked onto the yacht with Aaron and made out with him half naked. She slapped the magazine shut and shoved it under her bed. "I'm just sorry my relationship with Aaron ended the way it did. I acted like an idiot on Thursday in front of half my friends and Harry Darby and any important music people he invited that night."

"Oh, Tracie, it wasn't that bad. Everyone gets upset sometimes and does embarrassing things. And at least it's over with Aaron, thank God."

Tracie nodded. But she wasn't as relieved as Sienna was. Yes, Aaron was a jerk. But he was also incredibly handsome and sexy, and he had his loving moments too. Sienna didn't know his sweet side like Tracie did. Aaron always said she was the most gorgeous girl he'd ever seen, and he used to act like he really meant it. The night she had lost her virginity, he had switched on his bedside lamp to stare at her, so hard and so long she became uncomfortable and looked away. But then he turned her face toward his, begging her to let him gaze at her, telling her it was unfair that one girl should possess the world's bluest eyes and softest skin and prettiest lips, when most other girls didn't have even one feature as special as hers. And then he'd kissed her again, and moved his hands across her body. Oh, God, she missed him.

Tracie's cell phone rang. It happened to be in her purse, which happened to be right beside her, as it had happened to be ever since Thursday night. She hurriedly scooped up her phone.

Her eyes darted to the screen identifying the caller. Aaron.

She kept staring at it. If he was so awful, then why was she so happy he called?

"Who's that?" Sienna asked, her tone sounding accusatory.

Tracie didn't respond to Sienna's question. If she had, she knew just what Sienna would have said: *Don't answer that.* But was it so bad to talk things out? After all, she and Aaron had once been very close.

She turned away from her friend and murmured into the phone, "Aaron?"

"It's good to hear your voice," he said, echoing her thoughts. "I miss you, babe. My parents just went out, and Lily's at Mark's house. It's Saturday and I have the whole place to myself."

Did he really miss her or did he want to get laid? "Where's Whitney?" Tracie asked. Her voice came out bitter and snide, but she didn't care. Her boyfriend had been all over another girl at her performance; she should be bitter and snide.

"Damn, girl," Sienna said. "Don't tell me it's Aaron."

Tracie cupped her hands over the mouthpiece to block out her friend's remarks.

"Whitney's nothing to me," Aaron scoffed. "Just a friend with benefits, you know?"

"No. I don't know." She knew what a friend with benefits was, but she didn't know how Aaron could have one while he was going out with her. "Haven't I given you enough 'benefits'?"

"Yeah. Fantastic benefits. I'll pick you up at your house, Tracie, or you can come over. I'll get some beer."

Tracie suspected that he thought her "I don't know" meant that she didn't know whether to see him tonight. Actually, she admitted to herself, it did kind of mean that.

"Hang up," Sienna urged.

Tracie walked to the opposite corner of her bedroom, but Sienna said, "Hang up," again, this time louder.

"Can I call you back in a few minutes?" Tracie asked Aaron.

"No need to. I'll drive over. I'm leaving right now."

"No," Tracie said. But he'd already clicked off the phone.

"I can't believe you just talked to Aaron," Sienna said. "Did you already forget about him bringing Whitney Lowell to Waves and dancing with her right in front of your face? It's been less than forty-eight hours since he did that. He's a jerk, Tracie."

She sighed. "I know he's a jerk. And we're through. Really. But I'm not over him yet. I need—what do you call it?—closure. I have to talk to him, to tell him how much he hurt me, so I can get that out of the way and move on with my life."

"You're not going to see him again, are you? Why don't you just send him an e-mail or write him a letter or something?"

"He's on his way over."

Sienna shook her head. "Oh, honey, you know you'll just wind up in bed with him."

"I will not." She didn't think so, anyway. "I just have to talk to him for a few minutes. Once I tell Aaron off, I can move on." She wasn't sure about that, but she did know she had to see him.

"Tell him we'll meet him at Starbucks," Sienna said.

"We?"

"Yeah, we. I'll support you, give you a shoulder to cry on, and make sure you guys don't end up having sex."

"We won't," Tracie said.

"Call him and tell him the plan's changed, that you'll meet up at Starbucks. I can call him if you want. What's his cell phone number?"

Tracie picked up her phone. "Fine. I'll tell him. But you wait in the car for me, okay? I'd look so needy if I couldn't seem to face him alone."

Sienna agreed to have Tracie go into Starbucks by herself, and Tracie called Aaron to tell him the new plan. After Tracie quickly combed her hair and refreshed her lipstick, her friend drove her to meet Aaron.

But he didn't show up. She sat at a small table, stirring her latte and looking out the window for his Porsche. It was nowhere in sight. What was taking him so long? He said he'd meet her just as soon as he picked up some beer. She had told Sienna that she'd probably be at Starbucks for less than ten minutes. The fact that she had been waiting for Aaron for almost a half hour probably confirmed to Sienna that he was a jerk. She could just make out Sienna's car, parked in the back of the lot. She imagined her friend inside, looking for Aaron's Porsche just as she was doing, except that Sienna probably hoped it wouldn't appear.

His car finally sped into the lot. He parked right at the entrance to Starbucks. Tracie told herself to stay strong. But she didn't feel strong when she saw him come in. Why did Aaron have to be so handsome? Why did he have to smile? He knew she loved his big-toothed, cocky grin. And why did he have to wear that tight T-shirt that showed off his muscular body?

He came right to her table, bent down, and tried to kiss her.

She pushed him away. "I didn't come here to make out with you." She took a deep breath before continuing. "Aaron, you broke my heart." On the way over, Sienna had made her practice what she was going to say. "You took all the happiness I felt onstage with my band and my music and turned it into anger and humiliation. I want to tell you now, in person, that you hurt me and that I don't want to see you anymore." It felt good to get it out just like she'd practiced it.

He sank to the chair opposite hers, rested his chin on his hands and his elbows on the table, and looked at her with wide puppy-dog eyes. "Your heart is broken, so you want to break my heart too? Congratulations, Tracie. You're succeeding, probably beyond your wildest dreams." He sat up and clutched his chest. "My heart feels like it's just been sprayed full of buckshot. It's in a thousand jagged pieces. My whole body is torn up inside."

His heart. His body. God, he was so handsome. And more sensitive than he'd let on before. She had thought she'd enjoy telling him off, but she felt torn up too now. What was she doing here, anyway? It was cruel of her to get his hopes up on the phone and invite him out for coffee, only to break up with him now.

No, Tracie. Picture him last Thursday night, dancing with Whitney as if they were lovers, right in front of you. Talk about cruel! "I'm not changing my mind," she said. "We're through with each other."

"But, Tracie, I can't be through with you. My heart will never be through with you." His voice quivered. "Listen. Whitney Lowell came on to me, really strong. I should have resisted her. Now that you've broken my heart, I realize you're the only one for me. I'm done with other girls. They can't compare to you, anyway, Tracie, because you're the most gorgeous girl in the world. What can I do to get you back?"

"Nothing. It's too late." Tracie forced herself to stand up.

"Good-bye, Aaron." She made herself walk away. The door felt so heavy. But she pushed it open and left Starbucks, stopping just outside the building. The air was misty and gray, almost as foggy as her thoughts right now. She knew she should keep going, right to the end of the parking lot, to Sienna's car. Sienna would tell her that she'd done the right thing. She'd call Aaron a jerk again. She would be right.

Or would she? Tracie stood by the door, her mind racing but her body not moving. What if Sienna was overreacting about Aaron? Maybe he wasn't the jerk she made him out to be. Sienna had never liked Aaron, from the first time she ever met him. Being Lily's brother probably didn't help his case with her either. She must have been distrustful of guys, anyway, after Mark had spurned her. And Sienna probably knew she'd have more time with her if Aaron weren't in the picture. She should take Sienna's advice with a huge grain of salt.

Maybe Aaron deserved a second chance. Whitney Lowell was a strong girl—bossy, demanding, probably used to getting whatever she wanted. Was it totally Aaron's fault that Whitney had mauled him? She probably just caught him at a weak moment. And as he said, now that he realized how much he loved Tracie—well, he hadn't said *love* in so many words, but he sounded like he meant it—now that his heart had been broken, he would change. Why was she walking away from the most exciting thing that had ever happened to her, from the guy she loved, who no doubt loved her back?

She pulled open the door and returned to Starbucks.

Aaron wasn't sitting at the table anymore. Instead, he stood leaning against the pickup counter. His face was just inches from the barista, a tall Asian girl with a narrow face and long, straggly hair.

Tracie walked toward him, but he didn't turn around. She stopped about two feet behind him, listening as he talked to the barista. "I'm not usually this forward." He bent even closer to the girl. "But I have to tell you, you're the most gorgeous girl I've ever seen in my entire life. What time do you get off work?"

"You bastard!" Tracie shouted. She rushed out of the café, through the parking lot, and into Sienna's car, where she slammed the door before sobbing in her friend's arms.

twenty-five

"Tracie, you forgot your cue again." Mark sounded perfectly calm. But Sienna recognized that his overly steady voice meant he was really seething inside. Mark was an intense person by nature, and he became even more intense when Amber Road rehearsed. Sienna knew that the band was his biggest priority, and that he couldn't empathize with fellow band members who didn't put their all into Amber Road. Tracie, especially, would not get Mark's sympathy, as he wouldn't easily forget that she'd ruined their prospects at Waves. "You have to come in when it's your turn to play," he told her, uttering each word with precision.

"Tracie's just being magnanimous, giving the spotlight to the rest of us," George said. "She's like one of Prince's backup singers, or Hootie's Blowfish, or Destiny's children. I appreciate your generosity, Tracie," George joked.

His new date, a plump girl with long black hair in a ponytail like George's, laughed. Sienna laughed too. She didn't think it was that funny, but hoped that Mark and the rest of the band would lighten up.

Mark glared at her and shook his head as if to say, *It's your fault for persuading us to keep Tracie in Amber Road.*

Sienna glared right back at him. Where had Mark been three days ago? Not helping Tracie, like she had been. He hadn't comforted Tracie for an hour in the Starbucks parking lot while she cried. He hadn't been the one trying to stop Tracie from looking at the rearview mirror while Aaron and the barista left Starbucks together, holding hands on the way to Aaron's Porsche.

Tracie had every right to be heartbroken. *And so do I, for that matter,* Sienna thought. Mark could glare at her all he wanted, but he was the guy who had dumped her for another band member.

Mark shifted his gaze to Tracie. "Let's start again. Tracie, let's go. You can do it."

Tracie shrugged. "I guess." But her rhythm was way too slow.

"Come on. This is a hard-rock song," Mark said. "We don't have a lot of time. George has to leave soon for his job."

George shrugged. "Dude, she's just a soft-rock singer in a hard-rock world."

Sienna thought about laughing again, but didn't want Mark to glare at her again. George's date laughed, however.

"A soft-rock singer in a hard-rock world," George repeated. "Hey, Mark, do you think you can do something with that song title?" George's date laughed again.

"We can't do anything unless we're all trying our best and focusing at rehearsals," Mark said.

Sienna wanted to tell him to give it a rest. But he and the other band members had been kind enough to let Tracie come here today in the first place. They could decide she'd blown her last shot and kick her out of the band right now.

Had she blown it? Tracie was staring at the wall in front of her and frowning. Mark's strong-arm tactics weren't helping her focus. George's jokes didn't seem to calm her. Sienna didn't know how to set her friend at ease.

Wait. Of course. Carter. He always used to make Tracie smile. When she was with him, she did well in school and at band rehearsals and everywhere else. He was a natural leader and a nice guy. Even Sienna smiled now just from thinking about him.

Since Tracie wasn't with Aaron anymore, what was to stop her from reuniting with Carter? It had only been a few weeks since they'd been a couple. If Carter came over right now, maybe Tracie would stop pining for Aaron and start being her old self again. "I've got to use the bathroom. I'll be back," Sienna said.

"What next?" Mark folded his arms. "We've spent more time fooling around today than rehearsing. "And George has to go in twenty minutes."

"Sorry about that," George said. "But if I don't work, I can't pay for my equipment."

"True," his date said.

George banged on his drum. "This stuff isn't cheap."

His date slapped her hand on his drum. "Not cheap," she said.

As soon as Sienna walked into the bathroom and closed the door, she took her cell phone out of her purse and called

Carter. He picked up on the first ring. What a relief to hear his friendly hello. "Tracie misses you," Sienna told him.

"Sienna, you didn't even say hi." Carter didn't sound angry. It was more like he was teasing her.

"Hi. Sorry. I'm stressed, okay? We're in the middle of rehearsal, and Tracie keeps screwing up. Everyone's stressed, in fact. I think Mark is more than stressed. I think he's mad."

"Thanks for sharing that, but what does any of that have to do with me?"

"I'm worried they're going to kick Tracie out of the band. I was hoping you could come to the rehearsal."

"Now?" He sounded irritated. "It's Tuesday, a school day. I just got home from swim practice, and I have a paper to write. Why don't you call Aaron Bouchet and have him over instead?"

"Tracie and Aaron are history, Carter. That was the biggest mistake of her life, and she knows that now."

She waited for a reaction from him. He was probably smiling and pumping his fist or something. But over the phone he said nothing.

She continued her pitch. "Like I said before, Tracie misses you. I was hoping you could come by. You always were a good influence on her."

There was a pause. "So I'm supposed to do charity work for her? After she dumped me for that jerk?"

When he put it that way, it sounded as if Sienna were a terrible person for even calling him in the first place. But then she thought of her best friend, crying in the Starbucks parking lot on Saturday and staring forlornly at the wall of Mark's garage today. "Tracie's such a mess," she told Carter. "I wouldn't call unless I was really worried about her."

"You're a good friend, Sienna. I hope Tracie appreciates you. She shouldn't take you for granted like she did with me." He sighed. "Okay, I'll drive over."

Phew!

"I don't know if my coming by will do any good, though," Carter said.

"Oh, I think it might." At least it would do Sienna good. "Thanks a lot."

After they hung up, Sienna closed her eyes and remembered their double dates. Just last month, she and Mark and Tracie and Carter had driven to Carlsbad to hear this band that was supposed to be good. The group turned out to be lame and derivative. They'd left early and gone to a frozen yogurt place instead. Carter did imitations of the lead singer copying everyone from Mick Jagger to Seal. They laughed so hard. Tracie had spilled her frozen yogurt onto her lap and Sienna had snorted soda out her nose, which made everyone laugh even harder. Damn, those were good times—a lot more fun than drinking on the beach with the Bouchet jerks. It wasn't just Tracie who missed Carter. Sienna missed him too.

Things didn't improve after Sienna returned to the garage. Tracie dropped her pick, spending a long time on the ground looking for it while Lily said, "For God's sake, just use another one. We're all waiting for you." Then when Tracie found it, finally, she played the guitar almost like a beginner, much too slowly for the tempo of the song.

Carter arrived quickly. He must have jumped in his car as soon as he hung up the phone, and raced over. *He's a good guy,* Sienna thought.

Tracie's first reaction was to cock her head and ask, "What are you doing here?" She seemed more confused than happy.

"Just came to say hi, that's all," Carter said with a transparently fake casualness.

"Hi," Tracie said, as if they were doing perfectly fine without him.

"It's great to see you." Sienna smiled at him.

Tracie sighed, then studied the written lyrics next to her.

They started a new song. "Come on, Tracie, put in a little effort," Mark complained. Once again, Tracie was playing too slowly.

"I'm preoccupied, okay?" she said. "The guy I thought was the love of my life totally hurt me."

"Oh, Tracie," Carter said. "You're the one who broke up with me."

"Huh? I was talking about Aaron."

Ouch. Carter's eyes half-closed and his shoulders sagged. *It's like Tracie's breaking up with him all over again*, Sienna thought.

"He hurt me so bad," Tracie continued. "And now you show up, as if I need a rebound guy."

Carter straightened his body and thrust out his chin. "Don't talk to me like that, Tracie."

Lily stamped her foot. "I thought this was supposed to be a band rehearsal, not a stupid soap opera. Why is it that wherever Tracie goes, drama follows?"

"That was uncalled for," Sienna muttered. Lily could be such a bitch. She couldn't believe Mark preferred Lily over her.

"It was your brother who did this to me!" Tracie shouted at Lily. "You must have known he was a player. Why didn't you warn me?"

Mark took a step toward Lily. "Girls—"

"Oh, blame this on me," Lily interrupted. She spoke calmly,

as if to highlight that Tracie was out of control. "You ruined our big chance at Waves, Tracie, but somehow everything's *my* fault?"

"Your brother ruined my life!" Tracie shouted.

"For God's sake, pull yourself together," Lily told her. "We only voted to keep you in the band because Sienna said you wouldn't have another fit. And here you go again."

Sienna hadn't liked Lily before, but now she absolutely hated her.

"Sienna, you guys were talking about me behind my back?" Tracie glared at her.

How can she be angry at me? Sienna thought. *I was the only person sticking up for her at first.* She gritted her teeth. Without her efforts, Tracie wouldn't even be rehearsing here today. "We all want what's best for you," she told Tracie. "We know this is just temporary, that things will get better for you. We all agreed to keep you in the band."

Tracie shook her head. "I can't believe you had this discussion without me. What did you do, have a huge secret meeting behind my back? And you." She pointed to Carter. "Someone asked you to come today, right? I bet Sienna did. Another talk behind my back, like I'm a child or something."

He crossed his arms. "Believe me, Tracie, I'm more than happy to leave. The only reason I'm even here is that Sienna said you needed me." He stomped toward the door of the garage.

"Wait!" Sienna called to him.

He turned around, shook his head, and walked out of the garage.

"I can't be late to work again." George stood up.

"No, you can't," his date said.

"I think my manager at Burger Boy is getting suspicious. I've already used the flat tire, dead grandmother, and bad hair day excuses." George walked toward the garage door. "Keep the peace, okay?"

His date walked behind him. "Keep the peace," she said.

George followed Carter out of the garage.

George's date followed him.

"Tracie," Sienna said. "Aren't you going to go outside to make sure Carter's all right?"

Tracie shook her head. "You're the one who invited him here."

"I did it for you," Sienna said before rushing toward the garage door.

Outside, she saw George and his date put on their helmets, jump on his motorcycle, and race away.

Carter stood a few feet from his car. Sienna called out to him and he turned toward her. His arms were still crossed.

"I'm sorry." She slowed down, caught her breath, and walked over to him. "I had no idea Tracie would react like that. She's changed so much in the last few weeks."

He shook his head. "Believe it or not, I'm tired of hearing about Tracie. She's acting as if she's the only one who got hurt. And Sienna, you act like that too. You're so busy worrying about Tracie, it's as if you never got hurt yourself by that stupid boyfriend trade."

Sienna suddenly realized he was right. She had lost Mark, but she didn't go jumping on his back during a performance or yelling at her bandmates during rehearsal. When Tracie did that stuff, Sienna had reacted as if it were totally justified. She stepped closer to Carter. "Maybe by focusing on how hard

Tracie has it, I don't have to admit to myself how upset I really am," she said.

"Tracie gets everyone's sympathy, but she's the one who dumped me."

"And Mark dumped me," Sienna added.

Now Carter took a step toward Sienna. "You know," he said, "the two people who lost the most in that stupid boyfriend swap were me and you."

"Not true," Sienna said. "Tracie lost big-time when she gave you up. And when Mark dumped me for Lily, he lost the best thing that ever happened to him."

"I like your attitude." He smiled for the first time tonight.

Sienna had forgotten how nice his smile was, lighting up his already shiny, clear blue eyes, turning his handsome face into a dazzling one. "I do get your point," she said. "Everyone keeps rushing to help Tracie. You and I do, especially. And she acts like we're the enemy. I'm so sorry, Carter."

"It's okay. I just wish you realized how special you are."

"Me? Special?" she asked, genuinely surprised. No one ever called her that. She liked it.

"But you're always putting other people before yourself."

She sighed. "I really screwed things up by calling you tonight."

"You know what? I'm glad I got to talk to you. Really." He smiled even bigger and she reciprocated with a grin of her own. Then he put his arms around her and they hugged.

It felt so right, as if Carter had figured out exactly what she needed now. Sienna realized hardly anyone ever hugged her now. Mark was usually wrapped around Lily these days. And it seemed that she was usually comforting Tracie instead of the other way around. Sienna rested her head on Carter's broad swimmer's shoulder and relaxed in his long, generous arms. If he weren't Tracie's ex-boyfriend, she might even be attracted to him now.

"How could you?" Tracie shouted angrily. Sienna lifted her head to see her friend standing at the end of Mark's driveway with her arms crossed.

"How could I *what*?" Sienna said, even though she knew exactly what Tracie meant. She dropped her arms to her sides and took a step away from Carter. "Things aren't what they looked like."

"You're so wrapped up in your own misery, Tracie, that you can't accept that other people were hurt by the boyfriend trade you were so eager to join," Carter said. "You might have had a hard week, but we've both had a horrible month. We deserve a little comfort too."

Tracie kept her arms crossed. "Don't pretend that making out here by yourselves is called *comfort*. Because you're sounding as sleazy as Aaron did. I don't know who I'm more mad at: You, Carter, acting so above it all as you lie to my face. Or you, Sienna, having the gall to summon my ex-boyfriend so you can fool around with him a few yards from where the rest of the band is trying to rehearse."

Sienna backed away from Carter. "I called him for you, Tracie, because I thought you'd want to see him. Carter and I are just friends." Good friends, she realized. Much better friends than they'd been when he was seeing Tracie. She had felt so close to Carter today.

"I can't believe the only two people I trusted anymore would do this to me! My best friend and my ex-boyfriend. How could you?" Tracie yelled again.

"Come on, Tracie," Carter called out to her.

Sienna said, "You're jumping to conclusions that aren't—"

"I can't take it anymore!" Tracie shouted. "Everyone hates me! Aaron, Lily, Mark. And now I find out that you two hate me too."

"That's not true," Sienna said.

But Tracie yelled over her voice. "I can't stand anyone! I can't stand this world!" She jumped into her car and drove off, her squealing tires sounding almost as angry as her words.

twenty-six

Sienna pulled her phone out of her purse and speed-dialed Tracie's number. She was frantic. Tracie had said, *I can't stand this world.* That sounded like what people would say before they left the world. The phone rang and rang. "Answer, damn it!" Sienna exclaimed. Even if Tracie wasn't thinking of suicide, Sienna didn't like that she was driving when she was so upset.

"I'm going to ask for help," Carter said before rushing into Mark's garage.

Sienna called her friend's cell phone again, but there was no answer.

Right after she hung up, Carter led Lily and Mark to her. "You think Tracie's okay?" Mark asked.

"She sounded really upset." Sienna wrinkled her forehead. "I wish I knew where she was."

"We'll all look for her," Mark said.

Sienna sighed with relief. Mark was a good guy at heart. Maybe with the four of them searching, they could find Tracie before she did something terrible.

"We're supposed to look for Tracie now? It's already getting dark outside." Lily tossed her hair. Sienna imagined herself with scissors, chopping it all off. "Sienna, you just said you have no idea where she is. So how are we going to find her car among the millions of them in San Diego?" Lily asked.

"If it's too much of an imposition for you, then don't help us," Sienna snapped.

"Please, girls," Mark pleaded. "We can narrow down our search by trying to figure out where she might be headed. Maybe we'll get lucky."

"The beach," Carter said. "Tracie loves the beach. In fact, when we were choosing colleges, she didn't want to be more than fifty miles from an ocean."

"Oh, that's right," Sienna said. "And last year after her grandfather died, Tracie told me she drove to the beach to take a long walk on the shore."

"Let's go," Mark said.

"All of us?" Lily asked.

"No. Only those of us with an ounce of compassion." Sienna shook her head.

Lily stared at Sienna with her eyebrows furrowed and her hands on her hips. Sienna glared right back at her.

Mark put his arm around Lily. "You can ride with me."

Was he completely blinded by Lily's pretty face and long hair? Whatever. Sienna had more important things to think about now, namely finding Tracie. "Let's go," she urged.

"Carter and Sienna," Mark said. "You can follow my car.

We can meet at the shore and talk about how best to search for Tracie." At least *he* was focused on Tracie.

The ride in Carter's car was quiet. As she sat next to him, Sienna understood why Tracie might have thought she and Carter were more than just friends. She pictured him standing by his Prius tonight, holding her in his strong arms in the soft, dusky air.

She shook the vision from her mind. What if their hug tonight led Tracie to do something terrible? Sienna would never forgive herself. "You think she's okay?" she asked Carter.

"If she's not, I'll never forgive myself."

She wanted to hug him again, or at least comfort him with words. But the hug had caused all their troubles; and if she tried to talk right now, she'd probably cry. She turned on the radio. An old blues ballad played. Very appropriate. A woman sang despairingly about being double-crossed. Sienna hoped Tracie wasn't listening to the same music tonight.

As they approached the beach, Sienna couldn't help thinking that the last time she'd been to the ocean at night had been when they'd arranged to trade boyfriends. She wondered if Tracie would remember that too and be even more upset.

They hurried out of the car to join Mark and Lily. It was so dark and the shoreline was so vast. How would they ever find Tracie? She might not even be here, anyway. Maybe she was safely in her house, in bed. Sienna called her again, but still there was no answer.

"Let's split up," Mark said. "We'll go left and you two go right. I'll have my cell phone so you can call in case you spot her."

"I have a couple of flashlights I always carry in my car." Carter handed one to Mark. Sienna couldn't help remembering

Tracie's complaint. "Carter's such a boy scout," she used to say sometimes when they were going out. If acting like a boy scout meant being able to find Tracie, then Sienna considered it a good quality.

The group set out in opposite directions. "It's so dark here," Sienna told Carter as they inched forward on the sand.

"I can't let you walk alone. I don't want to have to search for Tracie *and* you." He took her hand.

She was surprised by how much she liked the feel of it. He was such a nice guy, she supposed, that she had always assumed he was soft and kind of weak. But he gripped her hand so firmly, she felt protected and safe.

She shook her head. What in the world was she doing? She was supposed to be looking for Tracie, who had gotten upset in the first place because she'd seen Carter and Sienna hugging. Sienna didn't even want to imagine what she'd do if she saw them holding hands tonight too. Their reason for walking at the beach was to prevent Tracie from doing something reckless. It was not supposed to be merely an opportunity to hold hands.

"I can't help thinking that this is the beach that got Tracie in trouble before," Carter said. "It was here that you guys decided to trade boyfriends."

His voice sounded so sad, Sienna felt like hugging him again. But she wouldn't be foolish enough to try that now. "I didn't want to trade boyfriends," she said. "I even tried to stop Tracie from drinking beer that night. But you know her. She has a mind of her own."

"I *thought* I knew her." Carter shone his flashlight at the ocean. "What about the trade? Do you think Tracie really wanted to do it?"

"It was all Lily's idea," Sienna said. To protect Carter's

feelings, she didn't tell him that Tracie had been gushing over Aaron before they got to the beach that day, and had leaped at the opportunity to hook up with him.

"I'm so worried about her." Carter's voice was choked up. "The crazy thing is, I think I'm almost over her, as a girlfriend, anyway. But she'll always be my friend. Even when she was with Aaron and I was jealous and mad, I never stopped worrying about her."

Carter was so sweet. Sienna wondered if Mark still thought of her as a friend. Mark probably rarely thought of her at all, unless it was as a member of Amber Road. And here Carter was, anxiously searching for Tracie despite the fact that she'd treated him terribly the last few weeks.

"I hope Tracie didn't do anything stupid," Carter said. "She's not a good swimmer and there's an undertow tonight."

Sienna grimaced. Walking next to her, Carter was desperately worried about Tracie. Meanwhile, she had been thinking about Carter and Mark and herself. She should be ashamed. Maybe if she had paid more attention to Tracie, her friend wouldn't have run off. Where was Tracie? She hoped she wasn't doing anything desperate.

twenty-seven

Tracie stood on the sand. She was tired of walking. Really, she was tired of everything—school, Carter, Aaron, the band, her alleged friends, her life. She had gone to the beach to clear her mind, but she'd just gotten even more anxious. Of course, she'd also drunk close to half a bottle of champagne.

She wondered how she'd ever make it back to her car. Even if she was able to walk all the way back, she shouldn't drive. She took another swig of champagne. The bottle had been stashed in her car since Thursday. She had hoped to celebrate the Waves performance with Aaron. Ha! There certainly was no cause for celebration that night. And there had been nothing to be happy about since.

She sat on the sand and crossed her legs. For the last few days she'd been really tired, but tonight she felt completely exhausted. She took another drink, then set down the bottle in front of her. She crossed her arms in an attempt to stave off the chilly wind. But that didn't stop her from shaking. She imagined her shivering was not just from the weather, but also from how she felt—sad, afraid, desperate.

She wondered how cold the water was tonight. What would it be like to swim in the ocean when it was so late and so dark? The water was probably freezing. But the sand was cold too. And she hurt so much anyway now, maybe the hard slap of the waves would make her forget her anguish. She took off her socks and shoes. Then she drank more champagne.

The ocean roared, but otherwise there were no sounds. She was all alone. Probably nobody was even looking for her. Her parents had tickets to the opera in L.A. tonight and said they'd be out late. None of her so-called friends cared about her. In fact, they had all turned on her. She drank more champagne. She couldn't trust anyone. It was over with Aaron, Sienna was seeing Carter, and now her own band was holding secret meetings to try to kick her out. They couldn't wait to get rid of her. But they'd sure feel guilty if she drowned in the ocean.

She pressed the champagne bottle into the sand and started walking toward the water. She would keep walking, into the ocean, farther and farther, until she could no longer stand. Picturing herself awash in the waves felt more comforting than scary. She'd let them take her where they wanted to go. She wondered how long she'd survive in the ocean. Perhaps she'd become a mermaid and swim away from her landlocked failure of a life. Maybe she'd find things better in the water. Anything would be an improvement over what her life here had become. Perhaps she would drown. That would also be an improvement.

She came to the edge of the ocean and dipped her toes in.

It was even colder than she'd imagined. She hesitated. Maybe she should return to the soft sand, try to make it back to her car. She could lie down in the backseat and rest inside until morning.

And then what? Return to her parents, whose panic over her whereabouts would turn to anger as soon as they saw her? Go to school to watch Aaron making moves on other girls, and Sienna and Carter hugging each other in the hallways? Face Lily's haughty sneers, and, worst of all, her own massive disappointment in herself? Spend the remaining school year, maybe the rest of her life, without a boyfriend or a band?

Tracie walked into the ocean and didn't stop.

twenty-eight

Mark shone his flashlight all around the shore before pointing it at the ocean. He wouldn't be able to forgive himself if something happened to Tracie. She was an anxious girl anyway, who had gone through an especially hard time after her breakup with Aaron. Why did Mark have to push her so hard at band rehearsal today? He'd been venting his frustration the entire time, shaking his head, admonishing her, telling her she had to do better. Was the performance of a band worth sacrificing the life of a friend? "Tracie!" he called. "Where are you?" But his voice barely carried over the loud, angry ocean.

Lily squeezed his hand. "When you called Tracie's name just now, you sounded terrified."

"She's my bandmate, my good friend," he said.

"Mine too, and I bet she's just fine. You know Tracie. She can be a real drama queen."

Mark let go of her hand. "Come on. She's hurt. She's upset." How could Lily make light of this? For all they knew, Tracie was at the bottom of the ocean. "I'm sure all my criticism of her in practice today made everything worse."

"Oh, Mark, don't blame yourself," Lily said.

But he did. If only he hadn't been so heavy-handed, if he'd been more patient and kind, maybe they'd be laughing about the rehearsal right now over In-N-Out burgers or Rubio's fish tacos instead of searching for a body on the beach. "Sometimes I get so carried away with the success of Amber Road, I forget the band is just made up of five human beings with feelings."

Lily took his hand. "We all appreciate your hard work for the band. Without Amber Road, I wouldn't have met you, let alone started dating you. And we all want the band to do well. I remember every second of our performances at Waves. It was an amazing experience, until Tracie jumped offstage. Mark, you know she tends to be dramatic about things. But she was all right after that night at Waves, and I'm sure she's okay now too."

"I sure hope so." He shone his flashlight on the beach again. "If something bad happens to Tracie, I'll feel horribly guilty—not only as a friend who didn't help her sooner, but as the person in charge of her band. Amber Road might not survive this."

Lily stopped walking. "Amber Road seems incredibly important to you. But you're so close-mouthed about its name. Is Amber a secret girlfriend of yours?"

"Oh, Lily. No, it's not that." He moved closer to her. "Amber was someone I loved very much though."

"*Was?*"

"Someone from the past. A very important girl." His voice was so choked up he could barely get the words out. "She . . . died."

"God, Mark, I'm really sorry," Lily said. "You know you can talk to me about her."

It did feel good to talk about Amber, after being quiet about her for so long. He spoke to her silently. *Amber, if you can, please protect my friend. Tracie's a sweet girl, and so vulnerable.* He shone his flashlight on the water, almost hoping to spot Amber's reflection.

"Oh, man." There was someone, or something, in the water.

"Mark? Do you see Tracie?" Lily asked.

A figure was out there, far out to sea, swimming, or bobbing, really. "That might be someone in trouble. It could be Tracie!" Mark cried just before he kicked off his shoes and ran toward the ocean.

twenty-nine

Tracie was in over her head. She had made a big mistake and there was no fixing it now. What tore her up the most was that everyone would think she had committed suicide. But she had considered killing herself for only a few drunken minutes before she changed her mind. By that time, it was too late. She had waded into the water and then gotten in too deep and couldn't turn back. The undertow had pulled her farther and farther out to sea. Now she dog-paddled in the cold, dark water—her arms and legs aching, her body freezing, her breaths coming harder by the minute.

If only she weren't such a weak swimmer. It was all she could do to keep her head above water as the giant ocean waves and the harsh current grabbed her.

As a child, Tracie had hated swimming lessons, begging her parents to let her take guitar classes instead. She pictured herself as a little girl in her plaid bathing suit, her arms crossed, her voice whiny. She envisioned her mother ten years younger. It was like watching a silent movie. *I saw my life flash before my eyes,* people said who had had near-death experiences. Tracie must be near death herself. It was too late to wish she'd become a better swimmer. She'd always been strong willed, and now it had caught up with her. If she had listened to reason instead of acting stubborn and impetuous, she wouldn't have run away from band practice and waded into the ocean in the first place.

Oh, her poor parents. She hoped they would remember she was impulsive and not blame themselves. She hadn't even left behind a note. What would it have even said? That she had been played by a player and lost her former boyfriend to her best friend? But now she wasn't even sure Carter and Sienna's hug revealed anything more than their friendship. What a fool she'd been when she'd decided to walk into the ocean.

And now there was nothing to do but wait for her death. She was exhausted. Her legs throbbed with every desperate kick to keep herself afloat. Her mind was tired too. She'd driven herself crazy thinking about Aaron and Sienna and Carter. And all that champagne she drank on the shore just made things worse. She tried to cough out the salt water and the pain in her lungs, but she was too weak. The attempted cough was more like a raspy, choking breath.

Thank God. Her parents had come. They stood on shore, staring at her across the water. Her father rushed toward the ocean to rescue her. As she watched him run down the sand and into the water, she tried to wave her arms. But she was so tired she could barely dog-paddle.

Were those her parents? No, she was hallucinating. People

did that when they were close to dying. She looked at the figure starting to swim toward her. She must be imagining him. Her parents had gone to Los Angeles tonight. Her mother had said they wouldn't be back before midnight. They wouldn't even know she was missing now.

At least she had told her mother good-bye as she left for rehearsal. But she hadn't told her mother she loved her. If she had wanted to kill herself, she should have at least planned it better. *I sure know how to mess things up,* Tracie thought. *Even my own suicide.*

Maybe she should just stop kicking. She was going to die no matter what, so she might as well do it now before the pain in her arms and legs got unbearable. She deserved to die, after her ridiculous tantrum at Waves and again today at the rehearsal.

She stopped kicking. *I should let myself sink,* she told herself. *Better to die now than after a lot more suffering.* She couldn't quite stop her arms though. They kept pulling her up.

God, she wasn't ready for death. She wanted to make more music, for one thing. She wanted to go crazy on her guitar again, feel the rhythm in her body and in her heart, let the songs pour into her soul.

She started kicking again—hard now, even though she could barely feel her legs in the freezing water. *I want to live,* she said to herself. *I have to survive.* She put her face in the water and tried to do the crawl stroke, forcing her arms up and out, up and out, desperately trying to move toward shore. The pain was searing, as if her arms were on fire and every movement of them made the flames hotter and bigger. But she kept on.

Then she heard somebody shouting in the water between

her and the shore. A figure, a person—a real, live person, not a hallucination—bobbed in the water. It probably wasn't her father, but it was someone, someone strong enough to shout to her. The person was swimming toward her. He called out to her, "Tracie!" Oh, God, it sounded like Mark.

She peered at him. Yes, it was Mark! She tried to answer him, but she was so tired she couldn't get enough breath to talk, let alone shout.

"Hold on! I'm coming!" he cried. Tracie had never heard four better words in her life. She swam now with even more energy, hoping that her ordeal would be over soon, that she would survive after all.

He moved forward with big arms high above the water and a trail of white foam behind him, zooming toward her like a motorboat. As he approached her, he yelled, "You okay?"

She wanted to shout, *Yes! Now that you're here, I'm okay!* But when she opened her mouth, the only sound that came out was a weak gasp. So she waited for him, using her little energy remaining to stay afloat.

Mark grabbed her waist. He used his other arm to swim with her, slowly but steadily, toward shore.

"Thank you," she said breathlessly. She tried to kick her legs in sync with his, but she had lost all feeling in them. And her arms felt as if someone had sliced them open and dipped them in salt.

"Let's just get back to land. Thank God I found you." Mark continued to hold her and swim. Tracie was so grateful for him, his strength, the way he took charge of her, his good heart.

Finally they reached water shallow enough to stand in.

They walked toward the shore together, Mark pushing her forward with his hand on her back. "We're almost there," he said. "Just a few more yards. Keep walking, Tracie."

But every step was agonizing. She could hardly stand, or even keep her eyes open. "I'll carry you the rest of the way," Mark said. He picked her up and held her in his arms until they made it to dry sand.

She half lay, half sat on the shore, exhausted but ecstatic to be alive. Carter, Lily, and Sienna gathered around her. Carter wrapped a blanket around her. Lily hugged Mark, calling him a hero. Tracie felt flooded with shame. She didn't know why her friends put up with her. She'd broken up with Carter in order to go out with a jerk, ruined everything for Amber Road at Waves, and now she'd caused four of her friends to spend the evening searching the beach for her.

Sienna stared down at her. Tracie couldn't have asked for a better friend. "I'm sorry," Tracie tried to call out to her, but her weakened voice ended up not much louder than a whisper. "I'm sorry for everything." Her teeth chattered as she spoke. "I'm such a horrible person. I don't know why you keep sticking by me."

Sienna sat down beside Tracie and put her arms around her. "We stick with you because we love you," she said. "And we know you're not a horrible person. You're just going through a hard time right now, that's all. You'll be okay soon, girl, I just know it."

Tracie hugged Sienna back with weary arms. "I'm so lucky to have you." It was stupid to have accused Sienna of being involved with Carter. Sienna was always on Tracie's side. She and Carter obviously were just friends, both of them sharing a concern for her. Mark and Lily cared about her too. "Mark, you saved my life," Tracie murmured.

"I'm just grateful we found you," he said.

Tracie was wet and cold and nauseated and extremely embarrassed. She put her hand on her stomach. "I drank a bunch of champagne, plus I think I swallowed a lot of ocean water."

"You want me to take you home?" Carter offered.

Tracie nodded. "Please."

"You need a ride too, Sienna," he said.

"I bet Mark can drive me back," Sienna said, and Mark nodded.

Tracie knew her best friend would feel uncomfortable riding with Mark and Lily. She was so sweet to give Tracie and Carter time alone.

As Tracie sat in the car with Carter, she thought, *Just like old times*. Then she shook her head. It wasn't like old times at all. They weren't dating anymore, Tracie had been drinking alcohol tonight, and she was no longer a virgin. They rode in silence, which made Tracie even more aware of her shivering body and lurching stomach. She wasn't sure whether her nausea was from stress, alcohol, her ordeal in the ocean, the winding beach road, or the anxiety she felt next to Carter. How had her life gotten so bad? She used to have so much going for her, but she'd thrown it all away.

She put her hands over her face and started crying. Carter still didn't say anything. She didn't know if he was too angry to speak or just indifferent. His lack of response made her cry harder. She remembered that things hadn't been exactly perfect while she and Carter had dated. Sometimes he had seemed so reserved, as if he loved her as long as she was perfect. But if she showed emotion or a shortcoming, he would turn away from her. The longer he ignored her tears tonight, the more upset she got. Finally, she said, "Aren't you going to say anything?"

"Are you okay?" he asked.

"Dumb question. I'm half drunk, I almost died tonight, my stomach is killing me, I'm in wet clothes, and I'm freezing. Why would you ever think I'm okay?"

"You get mad at me for not talking. Then when I do talk, you yell at me. I can't win with you."

Tracie's sobs were now partly from anger. Aaron cheated on her and Carter let her down. She took in a few deep breaths to try to control herself. Maybe she would never find the right guy. The right guy probably didn't exist. "You think you're so superior with your good grades and your water polo team and your debating awards." Her tears were slowing, finally. "But you're nothing but a typical male."

"Hey, what's that supposed to mean?" Carter's voice was sharp and steely, a rare tone for him.

"It means that I'm so sick of guys right now. They just think about themselves. All of them."

"All of them? Mark? Me? So we were thinking about ourselves when we combed the beach for you tonight? Jeez, Tracie, get a grip."

She realized she was acting like a selfish, spoiled brat. She wiped her wet cheeks with the back of her hands. "I'm sorry. You and Mark are so sweet. It was just Aaron who was mean to me, and I should have known better. You always treated me well, Carter."

"Thanks," he said stiffly.

He had treated her very well, almost like a princess. She

had given up the best thing that had ever happened to her. And for what? A player. A two-timer. An ass. What a mistake she'd made. And now she was alone. She hadn't been without a boyfriend in years. She and Carter had gone out since ninth grade, and then she'd been with Aaron. She hated that she had nobody now. "Carter." She swallowed hard. "Do you think we could ever get back together one day?"

There was a long silence. Finally, he said, "I don't know." Could he have sounded any less enthusiastic about reuniting with her? A new wave of tears ran down Tracie's cheeks—tears of regret. She should never have ruined their relationship.

She swiped at her cheeks as they neared her house. Oh, God, her parents had better not be home. They'd pummel her with questions. She closed her eyes and tried to make up a story for them. Dating Aaron the past few weeks had improved her ability to lie, at least. "Listen, Carter," she said. "I think my parents are still in L.A. But if they *are* home, I'm going to have to fib to them and I'll need you to back me up."

Carter groaned. Tracie knew he hated to lie. She used to think that showed great character, but tonight it was just a pain in the neck.

"They'll ask right away why I'm wet. And they'll probably notice sand on me too," Tracie continued. "I'm going to claim that Sienna and I lost a bet and had to swim in the ocean together. We'll tell them you won the bet. Okay, Carter?"

"I guess." He frowned.

Luckily, her parents weren't home. The message on the answering machine said that they wouldn't be back until after midnight.

"Wait for me, please," Tracie called out to Carter in the

hallway. "I'm just going to my bedroom to get out of these wet clothes."

"All right," he said, ever the gentleman.

She undressed. She felt so empty tonight. God, she had almost died. She couldn't imagine getting any sleep, especially when she was all alone in the house. She didn't want Carter to leave her by herself.

Her body felt sticky from the salt water, so she decided to take a quick shower. She could put on her bathrobe afterward and offer Carter a soda. "Give me ten minutes, please," she called out.

"You okay?" he asked her.

"Just wait for me."

She was soaping off in the shower, remembering Aaron's strong hands on her naked body, when she came up with an idea to get Carter back. He might want to rekindle their relationship if they could finally have sex. It would be silly not to, since she'd already lost her virginity to Aaron. And she was so lonely. She needed someone, a guy like Carter.

She quickly finished her shower and toweled off, opened the bedroom door wide, and then lay on her bed, naked.

"You sure you're okay, Tracie?" Carter called.

She didn't answer. Let him find her here. He'd know what she wanted.

"Tracie? I want to make sure you're all right before I leave."

She fanned her hair out on the pillow. Aaron used to say she looked sexy like that.

She heard Carter's slow footsteps coming closer. He looked in the bedroom. Their eyes met for a moment. Then he dropped his gaze and quickly turned around.

"Carter!" she called, but he didn't stop walking.

He left her bedroom, closing the door behind him. From the other side of the door, she heard him shout, "Good-bye!"

Tracie turned over in bed, put her face in the pillow, and sobbed.

thirty

"Is everyone feeling okay?" Mark asked as he helped George set up his drums at the high school gym. He really meant *Tracie, are you okay?* She was the one they had to worry about. He glanced over at her again. Her face was sickly pale and she had puffy gray crescents under her eyes like slivers of moon on a foggy night. She obviously hadn't been sleeping well, but at least she was alive and with the band.

Amber Road was playing at their own high school tonight. It wasn't a big deal like performing at Waves had been. But there was still potential for disaster. Aaron might show up with Whitney, since both of them were students here. Mark hoped Tracie could control herself. Even if bad behavior tonight didn't have professional repercussions for the band, Mark worried they'd be embarrassed in front of their schoolmates.

"You guys are pathetic, you know that?" George's new date

said. While the band rushed to haul their equipment onstage, tune up their instruments, and organize their music sheets, she had been observing them from a metal folding chair close to the stage. She wore a low-cut black T-shirt printed with the slogan "Womyn Rule," along with black jeans tucked into tall, black stormtrooper boots.

"You think we're pathetic?" George stopped setting up his drums and walked toward her. "Patsy, darling, you can't mean that."

"Pathetic." She stood up and yanked his ponytail. "George, you seem happy—thanks to me in large part, I'm sure."

"I'm not so sure," Sienna whispered. Mark tried not to laugh.

"But the rest of you! You girls are supposed to fight the male power structure, not each other," Patsy admonished. "Lily keeps looking at Tracie and then tossing her hair. Sierra, you—"

"That's Sienna, honey."

"Whatever. You've been staring at Lily like you're trying to eject darts from your eyes."

"I have not." Sienna glared at Patsy.

"Sure you haven't, Sierra."

"That's Sienna."

"And Tracie looks like she's been trampled on by our male-centric society. We women need to fight for our rights!" Patsy raised her fist in the air.

Mark had always questioned George's taste in girls, but this one took the cake. And probably smashed the cake too.

George kissed her on the cheek. "You're so honest. That's why I'm crazy about you, Patsy. You should have seen this band a few weeks ago. We all actually liked each other. There were no jealousies or broken hearts, just love and friendship."

"Then what the hell happened?" Patsy asked.

"They played this ridiculous boyfriend-trading game."

"Boyfriend-trading?" Patsy asked. "You mean like if you were to hook up with Lily, and I got together with Mark?"

Mark grimaced. "God, no."

"Please, guys. What if everyone pretends the game never happened? Can't we go back to how we were before?" George asked.

"I don't think anyone can return to how they were before," Sienna said.

Mark looked at Lily, sitting cross-legged on the stage, softly humming as she studied the lyrics of their newest songs. He couldn't pretend their relationship hadn't happened, and he wouldn't want to. He was crazy about her. He'd never imagined his feelings for a girl could be so strong.

But as happy as he and Lily felt, Sienna and Tracie were probably at least as unhappy. And Mark detested the changes in his bandmates. How could they sing and play with one harmonious voice, when offstage their voices were colored with anger and jealousy, both spoken and unspoken? Was this Amber Road's last performance? They'd already totally screwed up the Waves gig. It would be mortifying if they couldn't even get themselves together for a high school dance.

He had to try the best he could. They all did. "Hey, guys," he announced. "I'm calling an Amber Road huddle. Everyone come over."

George's girlfriend put her hands on her hips. "You're going to talk trash about me, aren't you? Just because I'm a strong woman. If you want to insult me, buddy, just say it to my face."

"George," Mark pleaded.

George stroked Patsy's cheek. "Darling, Mark just likes to have these pep talks," he told her. "He's not only the bandleader, he's appointed himself head cheerleader too."

"Sis boom bah," Mark said. "Now come on, George, we need you over here."

George left Patsy to fret by herself so he could huddle with his bandmates.

Mark spoke from the heart. "I hope you know I love you guys. Every one of you."

"Especially Lily," George said. "Though you have to admit I have a cute ass."

Everyone in Amber Road laughed. Patsy yelled from a few yards away, "Are you making rude comments about my ass?"

"No," Mark said. "But we will if you really want us to." Then he got serious. "I recognize this isn't a huge show like Waves was, but we still have to try our hardest. There won't be any record producers or big-shot managers listening to us tonight, so we have no reason to be nervous. We can just have fun for a change and still give it everything we've got. We *are* the top band at this school. Let's remember that. And don't forget that our friends at school love us and want us to do well."

"Give me an A!" George yelled.

"A!" the rest of the band yelled.

"Give me an R!"

"R!" they shouted.

"What does that stand for?"

"Amber Road!" the bandmates shouted.

"Nope," George said. "Angst and Remorse, which is sometimes what I think this band is all about."

Everyone laughed again. "Hey, don't knock it until you try it," Lily joked.

The band relaxed. They even managed to kid each other and goof off, so that by the time the dance started they remembered why they had become friends in the first place.

And their playing reflected that. All their emotions and passions went into the songs this time instead of each other. Lily sang with great clarity and range, and, more important, with heart. George banged on his drums almost as heartily as his new girlfriend shook her fist and hollered. Sienna and Tracie raced their fingers over their guitars as if they were on fire. And Mark used the great spirit of his bandmates tonight to play the very best he could.

Then Aaron showed up with his arm around Whitney. She wore a red dress with a long cutout starting under her arm and zigzagging down to her thigh.

Tracie's eyes glinted fiercely. But she seemed to put her anger to use, fueling her energy on the guitar. She totally rocked, and Mark couldn't have been more proud of her.

He was proud of everyone in Amber Road. This time they weren't playing to impress important people or to climb a ladder to success. They performed tonight for the sheer love of the music, for their friends in the audience, and to reach that amazing high of five people totally in sync, all excited about creating wonderful sounds.

By the end of the night, their classmates were on their feet, screaming and cheering. Even the adult chaperones smiled and bopped in rhythm to the music. The band played three encores before running offstage and hugging each other. Crowds of teens, including their friends and people they didn't know, clustered around them to thank them for playing and rave about their performance.

Mark realized that Amber Road had succeeded. Even if the band never got a record deal or even another club gig, making fantastic music with his friends tonight was worth all the hard work, all the emotional mayhem, all the agony they'd gone through. Maybe they just weren't meant to work under pressure. It was okay, Mark decided, to set aside their ambitions of money and stardom. He put his arm around Lily, beamed at the other members of the band, listened to the adulation of their fans, and realized he was perfectly content to have played at a high school dance.

thirty-one

Mark and the rest of Amber Road were congratulating each other, thinking about other schools where they could play, and packing up their equipment when a man approached them. He wore a chaperone's badge. But at about thirty, he seemed too young to be a parent of a high school student. And if he was a teacher at the school, Mark didn't recognize him. He didn't look like a teacher, anyway, with his nose ring and unshaven look. "Great set," the man said. "I could see some of those songs hitting it big. 'School Bites,' 'Rock It Like a Rocket,' and best of all, 'Beautiful Girl.'" He clutched his heart. "That one's amazing."

Mark thanked him.

"You guys have a manager?"

Mark stepped toward him with his hand out. "I'm the manager. Mark Carrelli."

"Steve Guyda." They shook hands.

Mark thought the name sounded familiar, but he wasn't sure how he knew it.

"I have a niece at the school. She's a freshman, Haley Guyda."

"Somehow, the name Guyda rings a bell. But we're all seniors, so I doubt we know your niece," Mark said. "Nice of you to chaperone."

"Well, I did it partly for selfish reasons. Believe me, my niece wasn't happy about having one of her relatives hanging out at her first high school dance. I came because I heard your podcast and liked your sound. I'm a manager for a few bands in San Diego—Jaguar, Melting Pot, The Jay Hunt Sound. You heard of them?"

"Yeah. All of them." Mark couldn't believe his good luck. He knew Steve Guyda's name seemed familiar. He was a top local manager. Mark tried to play it cool. If he didn't contain himself now, he'd be shouting and jumping up and down. "Lily and I just went to the Gaslamp last week to listen to Jaguar. They're really good," he said.

"I sure think so. I got Jaguar a steady gig at that club. I'd like to help you guys get more club spots."

"Oh, man," Mark said. He looked at his friends. He loved seeing their weary faces light up with hope and pride. He introduced each one to the manager, skipping over Patsy, who scowled before introducing herself.

"Good to meet you all," Guyda said. "You have a lot of talent, and I like the way you get along so well together. I can tell you're close friends."

The band members looked at each other with half smiles. Mark knew not to mention their recent problems. But he had to ask, "Did you hear us at Waves, by any chance?"

"I was going to, but I ate some vile spicy tuna rolls the day before. I hardly left the bathroom for three days. I don't ever want to eat sushi again. But enough about me. To make a long story short, I had to miss your set at Waves. You guys still appearing there?"

Mark shook his head. He shouldn't have even mentioned Waves. If Guyda were to find out about Amber Road's antics there, he'd probably have second thoughts about representing them.

"We're going to play at Waves again soon," Tracie said. "In the next week or so."

Mark glared at her. It was one thing to not mention what happened there. It was another thing to downright lie about it. There was no way Harry Darby would ever ask them to perform at Waves again. He probably wouldn't even let them sit in the audience.

"Good to hear that about Waves. It's a cool little club," the manager said. "And there are lots of other clubs in San Diego we could approach. Orange County and L.A. too, if you don't mind driving a bit."

Mark nodded. "We don't mind driving." He didn't tell Guyda what he really thought, that he'd drive practically anywhere for a paying gig.

"I'd also like to help you make a professional demo recording in a studio. I like your podcast. It shows raw talent, but it was obviously done on the cheap. Let's spend more time and money and really do it well. If you work hard enough, I might be able to get you a road tour too."

"We can do whatever it takes to be a success," Lily said.

"We'll work it harder than a gold digger at a billionaire's convention," George said.

They all laughed, except Patsy, who said, "Hey. If women were truly equal, there wouldn't be any gold diggers."

"I just love how well you guys get along," Guyda said. "That's half the battle, you know."

Mark nodded again, thinking the word *battle* was quite appropriate. Then he turned to his bandmates. "You guys interested in this?"

"Hell, yeah, we're interested," Sienna said.

"All right!" Guyda acted as enthused as the band. "I'll send you guys a contract and information about myself. After you look it over, we can set up a more formal meeting. Sound good?"

"It sounds fantastic," Mark said.

Guyda shook everyone's hand and left the gym.

As soon as the door closed, Mark pulled Tracie aside. He said quietly, "I think the best policy regarding Waves is to play down the whole experience. We shouldn't tell people we're going to perform there again, since we know we can't."

"Harry Darby is going to schedule us for the next available opening," Tracie said loudly.

"What?" Mark shook his head. Tracie was really messed up.

"I went into the club this afternoon and apologized. More like groveled, actually."

Mark's jaw dropped.

"Girl, you got balls," Sienna told Tracie.

"The more I get to know you, Tracie, the more I like you," Lily told her.

"Girl power!" Patsy shouted.

"Thank you, Tracie," Mark said. "Man, that must have been really hard for you."

She smiled. "To tell you the truth, I was scared to death to go in there. But I wanted to try to make things up to you guys."

"You didn't have to." Mark put his arm around Tracie.

"Yeah, you didn't do much for me. I mean, besides saving my life." She smiled at Mark again. "Anyway, after I apologized, Harry Darby was totally nice. He said members of rock bands weren't exactly the calmest people in the world, and he'd seen a lot worse at Waves. Then he told me all these stories. One guy brought a bottle of vodka onstage and drank most of it between songs and even during songs. He ended up barfing all over his drum set during the show. And about six months ago, this folk band had a screaming match with each other onstage over what song they were going to play next. They couldn't decide between this song called 'Kitten Love' or 'It's All Cool.' Darby said he knew we had talent and he'd give us one more chance."

"You're the best, Tracie," Mark told her. He had always thought of her as fragile. But Sienna was right about her. She did have balls. In a feminine way, of course.

"This calls for a celebration," Lily said. "This whole night was awesome—a great performance, impressing Steve Guyda, and hearing that we can return to Waves. Let's party on the beach again. I brought a bottle of champagne. Tonight it deserves to be opened."

"I'll celebrate," Tracie said. "I might even have a beer. But I don't want to drink any champagne. I don't even want to *look* at a bottle of champagne."

Sienna patted Tracie's shoulder. "That's understandable."

"Totally," Mark said. "But we should celebrate our success. With a good manager, hard work, great talent, and a little bit of luck, I think we have a fantastic future ahead of us."

Lily hugged him. Mark thought he and Lily had a fantastic future ahead of them too. He just hoped the band as a whole could get along. If they drove up to Orange County and L.A.

like Steve Guyda had suggested, they'd spend a lot of time in close quarters. With Sienna still upset with Lily and him, Tracie emotionally unstable, and George attached to nutty girlfriends, Mark wasn't sure that Amber Road was strong enough to make it. But he hoped they could. He could always hope.

"Dudes!" George exclaimed. "My wildest dreams of being a rich, famous rock star may come true after all. In a few years I see us at an amphitheater, surrounded by a mob of screaming fans throwing their thongs at us and begging us to autograph their CDs."

"George. No offense," Tracie said. "But, please, for the love of God, stop talking about your wildest dreams. The last time you brought that up, everything turned into a mess."

The band members laughed. Mark stood with his friends, thinking of the pure joy this night had given him. He looked up for a moment and hoped that Amber was somehow able to experience their happiness too.

Amber Road
beautiful girl

I fell in love today
Down at the beach by the
    waves
And our eyes met
And the sun set
The sky above us turning
    red and gold
Then he kissed me in the fading
    sun
He said I'm beautiful and
    I'm the one

I don't want to be the most
    beautiful girl
I just want to be the most
    beautiful girl for you
I don't want to be the only one
    in the world
I just want to be the only one
    for you

I fell in love today
Down at the beach in the sand
Don't ask me how
I just knew now
Nothing's gonna take our love
    away
Then he kissed me in the fading
    sun
He said I'm beautiful and
    I'm the one

I don't want to be the most
    beautiful girl
I just want to be the most
    beautiful girl for you
I don't want to be the only one
    in the world
I just want to be the only one
    for you

If it's right, right now
Why should I slow down
Don't let me touch the ground
Tonight!

I don't want to be the most
    beautiful girl
I just want to be the most
    beautiful girl for you
I don't want to be the only one
    in the world
I just want to be the only one
    for you

And now a special preview of the next
book in The Band series. . .

The Band
holding on

Coming from Berkley JAM
August 2007!!!

Sienna stood at the railing, watching the yacht set sail on the Pacific Ocean. It was beautiful outside tonight, with hundreds of boats of all sizes and types moored to the dock, the stars sparkling under a sliver of moon, the waves gently lapping underneath her, birds swooping by and calling to each other every so often.

Sienna turned around and studied her friends on deck. Almost everyone she'd invited had been able to come. The girls looked fantastic in their glittery makeup and soft dresses and delicate high-heeled shoes. The boys mostly seemed uncomfortable, fingering their ties and moving slowly in their bulky suits, shiny tuxedos, and heavy dress shoes. Still, everyone flirted and laughed and some of them kissed, and they ate the seemingly endless supply of fancy hors d'oeuvres handed out by the straight-faced catering staff.

She'd been looking forward to her eighteenth birthday party for ages, and it was exceeding her expectations. She gazed at her parents, holding hands as they sauntered around the deck making sure everyone was content. *They wouldn't have much work to do on that front*, Sienna thought. *Even Tracie must feel happy tonight, finally.*

She watched Tracie and Carter once again. They were still at the bar. She had never seen Carter in a tuxedo before. He looked so handsome, like a leading man at a Hollywood awards show. And Tracie had never looked better. It was as if that dress had been designed and sewn just for her. Everything about it—the color, the cut, the fit—was perfect.

The beautiful couple, Tracie and Carter, wouldn't even be back together tonight if not for her. Maybe in a few years they'd get married, and she would be Tracie's maid of honor, and Tracie would thank her in a speech at the reception. She deserved Tracie's gratitude. Carter hadn't wanted to take Tracie to the party. Sienna had to convince him. He was a good guy, and she knew he'd take good care of Tracie.

After seeing Tracie in her gorgeous dress, talking with her alone in his car and on this romantic yacht, under the clear night sky with a light breeze, Carter would probably fall in love with Tracie all over again. He and Tracie had been standing together at the bar for a long time, barely talking to anyone else, including Sienna. Maybe they had already reunited. *Wonderful*, she told herself. *It's just what your best friend needs and wants*. She should be so happy for the two of them. She should. Unfortunately, knowing how she should feel and actually feeling that way were two different things.

Sienna turned away from Carter and Tracie. It was her birthday—*her* night. Lately she had spent too much time and effort worrying about Tracie. Tonight, for a change, she would enjoy being the center of attention. And so far, she really had. Everyone had complimented her tonight, calling her pretty and lovely and beautiful, and saying she looked just like a young Halle Berry. Carter had called her a princess and said she looked terrific. She realized, with a measure of guilt, that his compliments meant more to her than anyone's.

Her father walked toward her. She duplicated his broad smile. She wasn't used to him appearing so dapper. As a math professor at UC San Diego, he usually was more interested in writing voluminous proofs of complex theorems than buying new clothes. But he had listened to Sienna's mother and rented a tuxedo. The glossy black jacket added just the right shading to his soft brown complexion. He had even gone to an expensive hairdresser today instead of the barber he usually frequented in National City. Sienna thought she actually noticed hair product—mousse or gel—in his thinning, salt-and-pepper hair.

He kissed her on the cheek. "Happy birthday, darling. You doing all right?"

Her smile grew. "I've never been better. Thank you so much for throwing this party."

"Your mother did all the legwork. I just paid for it. Come to think of it, your mother did that too."

Sienna laughed. "Well, I really appreciate you getting all spiffed up for this."

"That was the hardest part." He smiled. "I miss my sneakers and old corduroy slacks. As long as I'm all gussied up, and have the privilege of talking to you alone for a change, without your friends swarming around, I'd love a dance with you."

"Oh, Daddy, that would be great."

They walked to the dance floor with his arm around her. *Thank God a slow song is playing*, she thought. She'd seen her father boogie last year at her cousin Rayshawnda's wedding—not a pretty sight.

Her face tensed up as she approached the dance floor. There were a few couples on it, but two of them attracted her attention. Carter and Tracie swayed to the music with their arms wrapped around each other. Would Carter ever dance with her like that? Sienna pushed the thought out of her mind. Next to them, dancing about as close as two people physically could without having sex, were her former boyfriend, Mark, and his new girlfriend, Lily.

"You okay, sweetheart?" her father asked.

She turned her focus back to him, or tried to, at least. "I'm great, Daddy."

Her father put his sturdy arms around her. As they danced, Sienna reminded herself how lucky she was. She had great parents, for one thing. She shouldn't be jealous of Lily, even though Lily was beautiful and had a wonderful singing voice and was breathing in Mark's ear right now. Even though Lily had stolen Mark from her. Lily's life was far from perfect. She had her horrible brother, Aaron, to contend with. And Sienna suspected that Lily and Aaron's parents neglected them. It seemed like they were always out of town.

The song ended, and she hugged her father and thanked him for the dance.

"I'm honored you agreed to share your first dance tonight with your old man," he said. "But I don't want to keep you from your friends."

"May I have the honor of a dance?" Carter asked, doing his best Cary Grant imitation.

Her mouth dropped open. She looked at Tracie, who remained on the dance floor where she'd just been with Carter. Now Tracie's eyes were no longer sparkling; they were burning. Her lips, colored with pink lipstick and darker pink lip liner borrowed from Sienna, were pursed as she stared at Sienna and Carter. Sienna knew her friend well enough to have a pretty good idea what she was thinking: *how dare Carter and Sienna dance together*.

Sienna frowned. It wasn't her fault Carter wanted to dance with her. She hadn't even been watching him most of the time she was on the dance floor. But she suspected Tracie would make up some sort of conspiracy theory and blame them both. Well, Tracie's insecurities wouldn't stop her from dancing with her friend on her birthday. "Thank you," she told Carter. "I'd love to dance."

He wrapped his arms around her. They were warm and strong and felt just right against her back. Her hands settled a little above his bottom. She stopped thinking of Tracie. She stopped thinking of anything except how he felt against her— very good, very, very good. She felt engulfed by passion. She closed her eyes, and when Carter leaned into her, she moved even closer to him. There was that aroma of his again—like spiced apple cider. She drank him in.

No! This was so wrong. Carter had just danced with Tracie. He was supposed to be Tracie's date. And Sienna was supposed to be Tracie's best friend.

"You're a great dancer," Carter murmured. "And you fit just right in my arms, like we were made for each other."

She dug her nails into her palm. "Tracie and I used to practice together in sixth grade. You should have seen us. We took turns over who had to take the guy's part." She would keep reminding him of Tracie, of her own relationship with Tracie. She would not dishonor her best friend. She would not be controlled by passion.

But again, there was that difference between how she *should* feel and how she actually felt. She felt good in his arms, as if she belonged there, no matter how much she told herself she didn't. If he weren't Tracie's ex-boyfriend, if Tracie hadn't wanted him back, if Sienna weren't a loyal friend . . . But she had to face reality. She could not have Carter. It just wasn't right. No matter how right it felt.

When the song ended, she didn't look Tracie's way, but she still sensed Tracie glaring at her with fiery eyes.

"One more dance?" Carter whispered in her ear.

"I . . ." She wanted so much to say yes. "Don't you need to get back to Tracie?"

"I suppose so." But he drew her closer to him and she could hardly breathe, let alone object. When she did breathe, it was to savor the sweet, warm smell of him. They danced again, and it was as if they were meant to dance together, as if the entire birthday party and arranged date and maybe even their entire lives were set up just so they could get to these moments of holding each other tight and swaying to the music and realizing perfection.

When the music stopped, she made herself back up a bit from Carter's embrace and look in Tracie's direction. But Tracie was gone. If it were anyone else, she'd hardly worry. But Tracie was so emotional. Last time Tracie had seen Carter hugging her—just as friends, though that hug had felt very right then too—she'd driven to the ocean and nearly drowned herself. What if Tracie did something crazy like that tonight?

Sienna wondered whether Carter was concerned too. He didn't seem to be. His eyes sparkled, warm and happy. His palms were firmly planted on her back and his shoulders leaned into hers, as if he and Sienna were dancing in slow motion.

But they shouldn't be dancing. There wasn't even any music because the band was on a break. "We need to find Tracie," Sienna told him. "I'm worried about her."

"Oh, Sienna," Carter said. "When are you going to stop worrying about Tracie all the time and start thinking about yourself?"

"She's my best friend. I have to help her." She saw Carter's point though. She wondered if Tracie thought about her feelings even a tenth as much as she worried about Tracie's.

But she wasn't about to turn her back on her best friend now. She scrutinized the dance floor, hoping to catch sight of her. About four yards away, Lily and Mark were slow dancing without music. Lily's body was practically glued to Mark's torso.

A few weeks ago, Sienna would have been incredibly hurt, and rightfully so. *It's totally tacky*, she thought, *to make out with a new girlfriend at your ex-girlfriend's birthday party*. But now she had come to realize that Lily and Mark had something special, something she and Mark never had, something that made them want to hold each other close like that all the time, the way Carter was holding her right now, in fact.

"We can't be standing here like this," she told Carter, "in front of everyone."

He didn't let go. "Everyone? You mean Tracie, right? And she's not here," he said.

"She should be. She came as your date." Sienna made her-self back away from him and his strong but tender arms. "She must be upset. I'd better go look for her."

"At your own birthday party? That's how you want to spend your evening?" Carter shook his head.

"She's my best friend." Sienna sighed. She didn't want to be involved in Tracie's drama tonight. She felt she deserved one evening in which she, Sienna, was the center of attention for a change. But Sienna had to search for her. If she didn't, she'd be too anxious about her best friend to enjoy her party anyway. "I'm just going to make sure she's okay," she told Carter. She began making her way through the people milling around on the dance floor.

"I'll go with you," Carter called out behind her.

As they walked, Sienna looked from side to side for Tracie. Now that Sienna was no longer dancing or in Carter's warm embrace, she felt cold in the windy night air. She wrapped her cashmere shawl around herself, wishing it were Carter's arms around her instead. There weren't many people left up here, and they were scattered throughout the deck. With the dark sky and the dim lighting it was hard to tell who people were, whether Tracie was among them. The moonlight shed some of its glow onboard the yacht, but the black sky dominated.

Sienna had never seen so many stars before. She felt capti-vated by the sight. "The moon and the stars look so bright against the dark sky," she said, staring up at them.

"It's beautiful, and so are you," Carter whispered, close to her ear.

She would not let herself be romanced by Carter. They were supposed to be looking for Tracie, not starting up a relationship. She shivered, partly from the chilly temperature, but mostly out of fear about where she and Carter were headed. *This is not right,* she lectured herself again.

"Are you cold, Sienna? You're shaking." His voice was so sweet.

"Cold and scared." And excited too, though she didn't say that. She looked into his glistening eyes.

"Let me warm you," he said. Before she could protest, Carter put his strong swimmer's arms around her.

She tried to make herself think about the morality of the situation. But the only thing going through her mind was how very, very good his arms felt around her. And then, without thinking at all, she tilted her head to meet his, and they kissed for a long, wonderful time.

Sienna thought she heard footsteps coming their way, throat clearing, shuffling noises. But she didn't care. All she was interested in was Carter—his warm arms making her feel cared for, his strong but soft tongue urgent inside her mouth, his hands pressed against her back, which she craved all over her body.

"Sienna. Sorry for interrupting you," George said from behind her.

Damn. She and Carter pulled apart. George and Dara were holding hands. George looked down as if he were embarrassed about what he had seen. Dara peered off in the distance as if she didn't want to get involved. Well, Sienna wasn't embarrassed. Happiness was nothing to be ashamed about.

"I . . ." George started.

She wished he'd hurry up and say whatever it was he found so important. Nothing could be as important as kissing Carter right now.

"I thought you needed to know. Uh . . ."

"Yes?" *Get on with it, already!* she wanted to shout.

"Well, Dara saw Tracie in the bathroom. She was really drunk and looked really sick."

"Again?" Sienna asked.

"Yeah. Like when she got so drunk that night we sneaked into the Jacuzzi, and Aaron met us there. Except this time she was crying and stuff," Dara said.

"Aaron?" Tracie had never said he was at the Jacuzzi with her last week. And Tracie hadn't mentioned drinking that night at all. Sienna had thought that they told each other everything, that there were no secrets between them. Why didn't Tracie tell her Aaron was at the Jacuzzi? "Did something bad happen between Tracie and Aaron that night?" Sienna asked George.

"I don't know. I don't think so. He drove her home from the Jacuzzi."

Sienna's mouth dropped.

"Tracie didn't tell you?" George asked.

"Nope." Apparently, she wasn't as close to her best friend as she'd believed.

"Aaron's not here tonight, is he?" Dara asked.

"Not unless he sneaked on the boat somehow." Sienna couldn't stand the guy. "There's no way I'd invite him."

"Well, I just thought I should let you know," George said.

Sienna sighed. "You did the right thing. Thanks. I'd better go check on her."

"Not the best way to spend your birthday party," Carter told her.

"I know." It was an awful way. *Tonight is supposed to be my night*, she thought.

"I'll come with you if you want," Carter offered.

"You can't. I think seeing you and me together would just make things worse." She turned to Dara. "Will you show me where you found Tracie?"

Dara nodded and Sienna said good-bye to Carter, and romance, and left the starry night sky to deal with her so-called best friend belowdecks. She found Tracie in the restroom, standing in front of the sink, gripping the edge of it for support, and splashing water on her pallid face. She obviously had just thrown up—and her new, beautiful dress had a long brown stain down its front.

Sienna clenched her fists, but stood next to Tracie and said, as nicely as she could, "Let me help you."

"Oh, you've helped me enough." Tracie was slurring her words. Her breath stank of liquor and vomit. "You two-faced backstabber. I told you how much I missed Carter, how I'd do anything to get him back. I believed you when you offered to ask him out for me. I didn't realize you were really asking him out for yourself."

"I didn't exactly offer. You begged me to ask him to my party," Sienna said.

"If I'd known you were going to dance with him in front of me like you two were having sex right there on the boat, I never would have asked you to talk to him."

"We didn't dance like that," Sienna objected, though she knew they hadn't exactly danced like platonic friends either.

"What exactly went on that night when you went to Juice Caboose?" Tracie started to fall, then steadied herself against the sink. "You've been so freakin' vague about it."

"*Me* vague? You didn't tell me you were with Aaron that night."

Tracie's fists clenched like Sienna's. "Because I knew you'd be all superior and snotty about it if you found out. Just like you're acting now. Maybe if you hadn't left me on my own that night, I could have handled Aaron better. But you were too busy running off with my boyfriend."

"*Former* boyfriend," Sienna said.

"Thanks to you," Tracie said. "Stealing him from me under my nose, all the while pretending to be my friend."

She hadn't stolen Carter. Had she? She'd have to sort out everything that had happened to figure out how she'd ended up with Carter tonight, whether deep down she knew they'd get together on her birthday, and whether it was such a terrible thing. How could the wonderful feeling of kissing Carter possibly be a terrible thing?

"You're not my friend," Tracie said.

"You're drunk," Sienna said.

"And you're a horrible, lying bitch!" Tracie shouted.

Sienna stomped out of the bathroom.